True Color

Kendl Paker

Contents

Chapter 1	1
Chapter 2	5
Chapter 3	10
Chapter 4	17
Chapter 5	25
Chapter 6	31
Chapter 7	38
Chapter 8	49
Chapter 9	57
Chapter 10	66
Chapter 11	81
Chapter 12	90
chapter 13	100
Chapter 14	111
Chapter15	119

Chapter 16   127

Chapter 17   137

Chapter 18   144

Chapter 19   153

Chapter 20   166

Chapter 21   183

Chapter 22   199

Chapter 23   210

Chapter 24   219

Chapter 25   228

Chapter 1

L izzy West -

The houses on the block whizzed past like a movie scenery. Some kids were outside playing in their front lawn. I looked down at the dark pigment on my arm and at the white pigment that covered my four year old sister's arms next to me. McKenna was sound asleep in her car seat and unaware of the thoughts that were going through my mind.

My older brother by one year, Cameron, sitting in the passenger seat next to my mom, was flipping through radio stations. Him and my sister would fit in this neighborhood, but I wouldn't, because I'm black and they're white.

Ten years ago, when I was six, I was adopted into the West family. Sometimes I forget that I'm adopted, because they all treat me the same, regardless of skin color. About two years ago my mom caught dad cheating on her. She decided to move from the most diverse and interracial neighborhood, to a completely white neighborhood. Apparently she wanted change, like mega transformation.

The car stopped by the curb. "Okay, kids, here it is." My mom said smiling to Cameron, then at me in the rearview mirror. I forced a smile back. The moving truck was already in the driveway and the movers were unloading the boxes.

Cameron and my mom got out of the car, leaving me trying to soak the neighborhood image in my brain. My brother opened my door and smiled at me. "Lizzy, aren't you gonna get out? The house seems pretty nice."

"Have you seen the people around here? They look stuck up, Cameron." I complained.

He smiled. "Well I guess you'll fit right in." I stuck my tongue out at him and rolled my eyes. "I'm just messing with you." He turned and walked towards the house.

I unbuckled McKenna out of her seat and picked her up gently so she wouldn't wake up. We got about halfway up the driveway and she began to stir. "Where are we, Lizzy?" She asked half sleeping.

"We're at our new house now, Kenna." With that being said, she fell right back asleep. GOOD CHOICE.

When I stepped inside, mom was grinning. "It's so spacious, Liz. Don't you love it?"

"Yeah..it's really great." I said.

She pulled Cameron and I into a hug. "I know it was tough leaving all your friends, but I'm sure you'll make new ones." My mom let us go and started roaming around the house.

The movers kept passing by with dozens of boxes so I set McKenna down on a couch and went outside. I glanced at the house across the street and

I noticed a boy looking out the window. When we made eye contact he quickly moved the curtain back.

Weird.

By Sunday we had most things unpacked by now. I was up in my new room arranging stuff. The room was big enough, a little TOO big actually. "Most circumstances I know my fate, but in this love thing, I don't get the game. Why does it feel like, those who give in, they only wind up losing a friend." I began to sing.

I got bored, so I went downstairs into the kitchen and got myself an apple. Then the doorbell rang. "I'll get it!" I shouted and heard my voice bounce off the walls. I opened the door and a girl was standing there.

She had her head turned to the side so she didn't notice I had opened the door. I took a bite of my apple and chewed. She finally moved her head and when she saw me, she looked startled.

"I-I thought I saw...wait..who...I" She couldn't seem to form a complete sentence. I stared at her and took another bite from my apple and chewed slowly trying to figure out what this girl's problem was.

Then it hit me. She probably assumed only white people lived here and probably only saw mom and Cameron.

"Uh.." She said slowly then smiled awkwardly. "Yo."

"Hi?" I said uncertainly. This girl was weird.

Her eyes went wide. "Oh! Hello. I'm Taylor. Sorry about that, I just thought you were from the city-"

"Because I'm black?"

"Um." She shoved a jar in front of me. "Here. My stepmom made these for your family. You know, to welcome you guys to the neighborhood."

I took it and eyed her suspiciously. "Thanks."

Cameron came up beside me. "Hi." He said to Taylor.

Taylor's eyes went from Cameron to mine. She seemed confused or maybe lost. "Bye." She said quickly.

"Wait." I said. "Just to lessen your confusion a bit, I'm adopted."

Her mouth formed a huge "O". I slammed the door in her face, handed the jar to Cameron and started to walk up the stairs. "Lizzy! Why'd you do that for?" Cameron followed me up the stairs.

"People here are so stereotypical." I took a bite from my apple again.

"How do you know?" Cameron asked.

"When I opened the door, instead of saying hello, she said yo." Cameron laughed. "It's not funny, Cameron."

"I'm sorry." He followed me into my room. "I noticed she looked a little.. caught off guard for a second."

"I bet all they teach at school around here is to be judgemental." I sat on my bed.

Cameron leaned against the doorframe and took a cookie from the jar and examined it. "Speaking of school..we start tomorrow."

"What!" I yelled.

Yippee I get to go to school with a bunch of snobs.

This will not go well. I guarantee it.

Chapter 2

B en Campbell --

School? Is mom nuts? I can't go to a school with shallow minded kids who think "yo" is a greeting. I was taking a walk around the neighborhood thinking about going to school tomorrow. I crossed my arms over my chest. Do I even know where I'm going?

I spotted a playground up ahead and went over there. No body was there so I sat on a swing. "I'm not scared of lions and tigers and bears, but I'm scared of loving you. I'm not scared to perform at a sold out affair, but I'm scared of-"

"You have a beautiful voice."

I gasped and whipped my head around. A boy close to my age was standing there smirking at me. He had dark hair and light brown eyes.

I frowned. "And you are.."

He stood in front of me now. "Ben. I live across the street from you." I eyed him suspiciously. He smirked. "How old are you?"

"I turned sixteen three weeks ago, you?"

"I'm seventeen. Are you going to start school?"

"No. I'm going to sit at home for the rest of my life and amount to nothing." I rolled my eyes.

"You don't have to be a smart ass. I was just asking a question."

I stood up. "Well you don't have to be a pain in the ass getting into my business."

"Are you all like this?" Ben asked.

I gave him a cold stare. "Don't ever talk to me again, if you are going to make racist comments. I didn't move here for any bull, and I didn't move here to make friends." I turned and started walking back towards my house. I know I'm going to hate living here so much, but for my mother's sake I'm going to have to just deal with it.

--

"Welcome to Whitefield High." The middle aged woman sitting at the office desk smiled genuinely. The name sure fits the school. When I walked in I saw a field of white people. Cameron had already been introduced to a mentor and was in class. I turned my attention back to the lady, her name tag said. MS. RUBINO, COUNSELOR. "I'm sending up a mentor to help you find your classes. She'll be here shortly."

Like clockwork, a knock came at the door and the same girl who brought cookies to our house walked in. I looked away and sniffled at reflex as a sign of disapproval. I decided not to give her a hard time, since she probably thinks my mafia and I are going to jump her.

"This is Taylor Vincent. She'll be your guide today." Ms. Rubino said.

I put on a big smile. "Oh we've met. Her dearest mother made my family cookies to welcome us into the neighborhood." I looked at Taylor and she looked shocked that I was being nice. "What a kind gesture." I put my hand over my chest. "I am very greatful."

The counselor smiled again. "Wonderful! I hope you have a great first day here." She handed me my schedule and locker number. "Come see me any time if you have any problems.

"I will thank you." Taylor and I walked out the door and the hallways were empty since classes were in session. We walked in silence to my first class.

"So are you excited about your first day?" Taylor asked, forcing cheeriness in her voice.

"Not really. Hey I'm sorry about slamming the door in your face the other day."

"It was yesterday." She said in a tiny whisper. I held in my laugh. "I'm sorry I made inaccurate assumptions. It was really rude of me. I'm really not a racist or judgemental person, you know? I just speak before I think, but like…"

"Okay, okay I forgive you." I laughed. She was wierd, but funny.

She smiled. "You have the same lunch as me. I can introduce you to some of my friends."

"Okay." We reached my first class, I was like 25 minutes late.

"You're in a Junior class!" Taylor squealed.

"I skipped fourth grade." I said.

She sighed. "Your so lucky, you get to be with hot guys and I'm stuck with the lame sophmores." I laughed.

When I walked into my class, which was calculus, every single head turned my way. Like I was a magnet or something. Geez, they act like they've never seen a black person before. The teacher hesitated before she spoke. "Hello, you must be Elizabeth West."

"I prefer Lizzy."

She smiled. "Okay, Lizzy, you can take that seat in the back over there." She pointed as if I was blind and couldn't see. There was an empty desk right in the front. Talk about racist. I rolled my eyes and looked at the class. I saw that kid Ben sitting in the front, smirking at me.

I slowly walked to the back of the classroom and took my seat. I kept looking at the clock praying that the bell would ring. The longer I stared at it, the slower it went. I put my head down on the desk. After a few minutes, the bell rang. Everybody rushed out of the classroom. Ben walked up to my desk. "I thought you said you were sixteen."

I didn't look at him. "I skipped a grade."

"Listen, I'm sorry about what I said yesterday. Do you forgive me?" I looked at him and he looked serious.

I slung my backpack over my shoulder. "Yeah, whatever." I saw Taylor standing at the door waiting for me. "Gotta go, see you later." I hurried out of the classroom.

"Were you just talking to Ben Campbell?" Taylor said excitedly.

I scrunched up my nose. "He's not that great, and he lives across the street from us."

"Yeah, but I never talked to him. He's so popular." She said. Then as we were walking I saw Cameron. We waved at and stopped to talk to eachother. He may be my brother but he's like my best friend.

"How's your day going so far?" He asked.

"A lot of stares but I think I'll get used to it."

He laughed. Then he looked at Taylor.

"You remember Taylor, right?" I said.

He nodded and gave me a look that said "Be nice"

Taylor and I continued to walk to my class. "I think Ben's got some competition now." She said randomly.

"What?" I had no clue what she was talking about.

"Your brother is freakin hot, Lizzy!" She twirled a strand of her brunette hair. "I just hope Erin Maguire doesn't see him."

"Who's Erin Maguire?"

We finally reached my second class. "You'll know her when you see her." I sighed and walked into my Anatomy class.

A short guy with a receeding hair line was the teacher. Again, all the attention was put on me. "Welcome to Anatomy." He said. "My name is Mr. Timmer. Take a seat anywhere you want." At least he gave me an option. I walked to a seat in the second row and sat down.

"I think she's in the wrong school, this isn't the projects." Someone behind me whispered. I turned around to look at biatch who said that. A girl with blonde hair who looked like a complete snob, sat behind me.

She smiled at me. I rolled my eyes and turned back around. I had a funny feeling that she was Erin Maguire.

She chose the wrong person to mess with.

Chapter 3

T aylor Vincent -

"This is Alex." Taylor pointed to a pretty indian girl sitting at the table. We were at lunch and she was introducing me to her friend.

I smiled "Hey, I'm lizzy."

"Do you want to be part of our group?" Alex asked.

"What group?"

"The outcasts."

"Thanks." I said sarcastically.

Taylor jumped in. "Well, Alex is an outcast because she's indian. You're an outcast because of your race. And me..I'm just an outcast in general.

I laughed. We ate our lunch and I spotted Cameron on the other side of the cafeteria. I went over to see who he was sitting with, and what do you know? He was sitting with Erin and her barbie friends. I stopped in my tracks and stared in disbelief. I can't let my brother turn into one of them. I approached the table slowly. "Hey Cameron."

He smiled when he saw me. "Hey Lizzy. What's up?"

I heard some girls at the table snicker. I snapped my head in their direction. "What's so funny?"

Erin rolled her eyes and flipped her hair. "I can't believe you know this girl Cameron. It's such a coincidence you both were new on the same day."

"I'm his sister you dipshit." I frowned at Cameron. "Why are sitting with these idiots?"

"Lizzy, you don't have to insult them." He said.

"Yeah Lizzy, be nice." I heard a voice behind and I spun around. Ben was standing there smirking at me.

"Oh look. It's Ben." Erin said desperately.

Ben rolled his eyes. "Yeah look, it's me." He said in an annoyed tone. If he didn't like Erin Maguire, I think I might start to like this kid.

Erin pulled out the chair next to her. "I saved you a seat."

"I won't be needing it." He said and I laughed.

Erin glared at me then snapped her finger. Her little pal next to her stood up holding a bowl of chilli. Before I could react, she tossed the chili right at me, splattering it all over my shirt. She put on an innocent face and put her hand over her mouth, "Oops. It slipped."

Ben looked surprised, but he wasn't laughing. I stared my brother in shock. He looked shocked as well at what just happened, but he didn't do anything. He didn't defend me. He was turning into one of them, I could feel it.

I knew if I stayed there i would have beat the crap out of her and I wasn't trying to be suspended my first day of school. I walked angrily into the bathroom while the whole cafeteria laughed at me. I was beyond pissed. If I could make up a word it would be furiopissed. I was furious and upset. It was so embarrasing.

I wet a paper towel and dabbed it at my purple shirt I got for my birthday from my mom. The bell had already rung, so I was already missing class. Through the mirror I saw the bathroom door open and Taylor walked in. "I'm sorry, Lizzy."

I shrugged. "It's not your fault."

"Those girls are so evil, they really are." She took off her hooded jacket and handed it to me. "You can wear this to cover up the stain."

I took it. "Thanks Taylor. You are a good friend."

She smiled. "So we're friends?"

I smiled back. "Yeah, now get to class. I'll be fine."

She left and I got most of the chili or whatever that thing was, off my shirt. I put on the jacket, zipped it up and walked out of the bathroom. Leaned against the wall outside the door, was Ben. "What are you doing here?" I asked.

"I wanted to make sure you were okay." He said.

"Really?"

He smirked. "No, actually I'm ditching homeroom."

I rolled my eyes. I actually thought he had a soft side to him. "Whatever." I started walking away.

"That was a little funny though." He said laughing. I flipped him off and kept walking.

I waited for Taylor after school in the parking lot. We were walking home together. While I was waiting, Ben pulled up beside me in his red corvette. "Want a ride?"

We lived like a block and a half away from the school and all of these spoiled brats drove home, what a waste of gas. "It takes like 5 minutes to walk home, and like 45 seconds to drive."

He stared at me as if waiting for me to make a point. I shook my head. "No thanks I wouldn't want to be part of the air pollution contribution."

"Aw you care about the enviornment. That's cute Lizzy." I rolled my eyes. "Suit yourself." He turned the radio on full blast and drove away. What an idiot.

Out of the corner of my eye I saw Taylor stand beside me. "Ready?" She asked.

"Yeah." We began walking, and started talking about school and Taylor told me about all the people I should stay away from. "Erin's top of the list, right?"

Taylor laughed. "Of course."

I heard a car honk and slow down at the curb. Erin Maguire rolled down the window of her lime green car and took off her sun glasses. Speak of the devil. There was a guy sitting in the passenger seat beside her. I got a closer glimpse and it was Cameron.

"Enjoying your little walk?" Erin said in a snotty tone.

I crossed my arms over my chest. "We were, until your hideous face came into view."

Erin still had a smile on her face. "This is the first day I've met you, and I already don't like you, Lizzy."

"Oh my feelings are terribly hurt, I'm going to go sit in the corner when I get home and cry my eyes out. " I took Taylor's arm. "Let's go." Erin drove away and I could already see her drop Cameron home. Yeah that's how close we live to the school.

I heard Taylor sigh. "I wish I could be more like you Lizzy. You know how to speak up and defend yourself. Whenever Erin insults me I just back down." She tucked her hair behind her ear. "I've known her for 8 years and I still can't stand up to her, and you've known her for like 7 hours and you are already her enemy." We both laughed. "That's beyond cool."

"Well, I learned how to be tough when I was younger. I was in a couple foster homes with some mean kids and I just couldn't take it."

"You're like my hero, girl." We laughed again. Taylor and I got to our houses then I asked her if she wanted to do homework together.

"Sure! It's so cool that we live next door to eachother!" She rambled. "Anytime we wanna hang out, we can, that's terrific!" I laughed.

My mom was still at work and Mckenna was at day care, so Cameron and I were left home. I ignored him when Taylor and I walked in and we went up to my room.

I attached my ipod to its speakers so we could listen to some music. I was sprawled on my bed, while Taylor was on the floor. I decided to mess with her for a minute. I scrolled to a Twista song and pressed play. A whole bunch of uncomprehensive words erupted throughout the room. I saw the look on Taylor's face and nearly exploded. Her head was down, but she had a look of confusion and overwhelming expression on her face. As if she were suffering.

I burst out laughing hysterically. I started rolling on my bed and accidently rolled off the edge and landed with a loud thud. It didn't hurt so I continued to laugh. "Lizzy, what's wrong with you?" I heard Taylor ask.

I kept laughing and pointed at her. "Your..hahaa..your face was so...funny."
I finally pulled myself together. "I guess you don't like rap music very
much."

Taylor smiled. "Oh, I'm just not used to it that's all."

I pressed pause. "I was just messing with you anyway. That was funny." She
laughed. I played an Owl City song.

Taylor gasped. "You listen to Owl City?" She acted like I just told her I can
read minds.

I smiled. "Yeah, my favorite's Hello Seattle."

Taylor's eyes went wide. "Me too! Woah this is wierd."

"I listen to rap, hip hop, and rock."

"That's cool." She said. My bedroom door opened and Cameron stood in
the doorway.

"What?" I asked. I was still pissed at him.

"I wanted to make sure you guys were okay." He crossed his arms over his
chest.

"Well you didn't seem to care when I got expired chili dumped on me." I
said with venom in my voice.

"Lizzy..."

"Look obviously we're fine, so you can leave now." I rolled my eyes. "Why
don't you go make babies with Erin." I muttered. I heard Taylor giggle.
Cameron stared at me for a long time. "Get out of here!" I yelled and then
finally he left and shut the door behind him.

"That was pretty harsh." Taylor said and sighed. "But, I'm gonna like spending time over here so I can check out your brother Lizzy. He's so hot, don't you see...." I glared at her. She laughed nervously. "Right, he's your brother and it would be wrong for you to think that way." A smiled crept on her face. "But I can think about him all I want."

I shook my head and looked down at my homework. "It's really hard for us to do homework together, when I'm a Junior and you are a Sophmore."

She laughed. "It's not my fault you are so smart." She got up off the floor and stood by the window. She gasped.

"What?" I stood beside her and Ben was outside with two other guys, who I guessed were his friends. I groaned. "Taylor, seriously?"

"Your brother's hot, but Ben's nice to look at." She was a boy crazed maniac. She grabbed my arm. "Come on let's go outside and say 'hi'."

"No way." I looked back out the window and one of the guys with him pointed straight at us. "Get down!" Taylor and I jumped onto the floor.

"Do you think they saw us?" Taylor asked.

"Duh, Taylor."

She got onto her knees and looked back outside. "Hey, they're gone." I got up also and the doorbell rang. Taylor and I exchanged a glance. "Uh-oh."

Chapter 4

C ameron -

CRAP. CRAP. CRAP. THIS IS NOT GOOD. THEY PROBABLY THINK WE'RE STALKERS WATCHING THEIR EVERY MOVE. TERRIFIC.

"Maybe if nobody answers the door, they'll go away." Taylor said. I heard Cameron's footsteps downstair on the wood floors and the door open.

I sighed. "Too late." There were muffled sounds downstairs.

"Lizzy! Some guys are here to see you!" Cameron shouted.

Taylor and I opened my bedroom door and peered out. "Uh, I don't know any guys, so just tell them to leave!" I shouted back to him.

"Lizzy, get down here!" Cameron's voice was stern. I sighed.

Taylor smiled. "Ooh, he sounds cute when he's agitated." I rolled my eyes. We began walking down the stairs with Taylor behind me. I stopped at a step and tried to see in theliving room. I saw Ben and his friends sitting there. Taylor leaned over my shoulder a little too far and I lost my balance and it sent us both sliding down the stairs with loud thuds.

"What the..." I heard one guy say. We heard rushing footsteps and all the guys including Cameron were staring at us on the floor looking like idiots.

I whispered to Taylor. "Good job." I said sarcastically.

She turned red. "My bad." She said quietly.

"What happened?" Cameron asked.

"We fell down the stairs." Taylor said slowly, and rubbing her leg at the same time. "My butt hurts." All of them started cracking up. After his little laugh fest, Ben held out his hand to help me up. When I stood up pain shot throughout my leg. I grimaced. Cameron helped up Taylor and I could tell she liked it.

"Ouch." I said rubbing my leg. I turned to Taylor. "Next time you want a glimpse just let me know." I said through clenched teeth. I grabbed her arm and we both limped to the couch in the living room.

Cameron gave us a wierd look. "You girls are strange. I'll be up in my room if you need me." He jogged up the stairs and about halfway he stopped and said, "I better be cautious, before I fall down the stairs." Him and the three guys burst out laughing like it was so funny. Then he finally left.

I glared at Ben. "Okay what do you want?"

"Well, these are my friends, Ryan and Kevin." He pointed to each of them. Ryan had blonde hair and blue eyes with dimples on both his cheeks. Kevin had dark brown hair and hazel eyes.

"Is that why you came here?" I asked.

"Actually we were bored, so I felt like stopping by to say 'hello'." He smirked at me

Maybe they didn't see us looking at them though the window. I smiled. "Well 'hello'." I stood up from the couch and walked to the front door and held it open. "And goodbye" I motioned for them to leave. Just then Mckenna came running through the door.

"Lizzy! Lizzy! Lizzy!" She chanted.

I scooped her up in my arms. "Hey, Kenna. How was day care?"

"I made a new friend! Her name is..uh..uh. Oh no Lizzy I forgot my new friend's name!" Mckenna exclaimed.

I laughed. "It's okay." I set back down on the floor. "Ask her again tomorrow."

"Okay." Mckenna looked at Taylor and the guys in the living room. "Are these your boyfriends?"

"I wish." Taylor mumbled.

Then my mom walked through the door carrying bags of groceries. When she saw the people in our house she had a confused look. I pointed at Taylor.

"This is Taylor." I pointed to the guys. "Cameron let these other barbarians in our house." I smiled sweetly. "Need any help?"

My mother laughed at shook her head. "Be nice, Lizzy, and yes I could use some help sweetie."

"We'll help you." Ben said and smiled. "You need strong men to carry those bags."

Mom smiled. "Thank you." I rolled my eyes. Kevin, Ben, and Ryan went outside to get the rest of the groceries and as Ben walked by he stopped and whispered something in my ear.

"You shouldn't push back the curtain all the way. It makes it less obvious when you stare at people through the window." He smirked and continued out the door. My mouth hung open in shock.

--

"So, how was school today?" Mom asked while we were sitting at the table having dinner. I didn't want to worry her, so I lied.

I smiled. "School was great. I made a new friend today."

"Taylor, right?" I nodded. "Oh, she is such a nice girl." My mom looked at Cameron. He didn't say one word during dinner. I wonder what's bothering him. Being liked by a bitch or by half the student body? I'm not sure which one is worse. "What about you, Cameron, do you like the people there?

He continued to look down at his plate. "Yeah, they're nice."

I nearly choked on my potato salad. I started to cough.

Mom reached over and patted my back. "Honey, are you okay?"

I put my hand over my chest. "Yeah, I'm fine." I glanced at Cameron and he was looking at me with a nervous expression. "I have a headache, so I'm just gonna go lay down." I washed my plate in the sink and went up to my room and lay on my bed. About thirty minutes later there was a knock at my door.

"Come in."

Cameron came in and sat at the edge of my bed. "Hey, mom wanted me to come and check on you."

I didn't really have a headache anyway. "Mmm." Was all I said.

"I've been thinking and what I did at lunch today wasn't right. I'm your older brother and I should have stuck up for you. I'm sorry, Lizzy."

I sat up. "I forgive you, Cameron" He smiled and we gave eachother a hug.

"That Ben guy's pretty cool." Cameron said.

"Yeah he's okay." I rolled my eyes. I reached across my bed and grabbed my notebook. "Well I'm gonna write some lyrics now."

"Okay." Cameron left my room and I stared the wall. I couldn't think of anything, so I put my notebook away and called my best friend, Julia, from back home.

"Oh my goodness! Lizzy, I miss you so much." She squealed on the other line. "How's school and everything?"

I sighed. "Awful. I'm the only black person in the entire school and the majority of those stupid kids are racist."I began to remember my life back in Cedarville. I was so happy there, and my neighborhood was diverse so I didn't stand out. Also, there were less stereotypical comments towards black people. I had friends of all different backrounds, white, Hispanic, asian, black, you name it.

"Aw, Liz I'm so sorry." Julia, being white, and knowing me the longest knew what I was going through right now. When she had moved to Cedarville, she had come from an all black neighborhood..and you understand the rest.

"Are there any hot guys you could be interested in?" She asked.

I laughed. "None whatsoever." She reminded me a bit of someone. "You know, you should come and visit sometime. I met a girl named Taylor and you two would get along great." They both shared a common interest: Boys.

Julia and I talked for about an hour more and then I fell asleep.

My second day was just as bad as the first. I still kept hearing racist comments, but I was able to ignore them. I had drivers ed seventh period with Taylor, so at least I had somebody to talk to.

"I have so many places to take you here, Lizzy. We have to go to the mall, there's always cute guys." Taylor added excitedly.

I laughed. "Is there any minute that you aren't thinking about boys?"

"Of course not. I dream about boys in my sleep."

So I made through another full day at school. Taylor and I walked home from again. It was mid October and it was very windy. My hair flew in all different directions so I pulled the hood of my sweater over my head. I was going to be screwed once it started snowing.

We reached Taylor's house and a woman was standing on the porch watching us. I waved and the woman just stared at me. "What did I do?"

"I'm sorry. That's my evil stepmom." Taylor said. "She's so rude."

I just nodded. "I'll just do my homework at my house. I'll call you later." I walked quickly next door and I saw a black Lincoln Navigator in the driveway. I instantly became really happy. I ran inside and I saw him sitting at the kitchen table.

"Dad!" I exclaimed.

He stood up and wrapped his arms around me. "Lizzy! You've grown since the last time I saw you!"

"I missed you." I said.

"I'm glad somebody does." He said sounding hurt.

"Where's Cameron?" I said looking around.

"He's not too happy to see me. When he opened the door his exact words were 'Why the Hell are you here?'" Dad ran his fingers through his hair. "He just stormed up the stairs and left me down here. I nearly got lost, this place is huge."

Uh-oh. Cameron never forgave Dad for what he did to mom. He doesn't even like talking to him anymore. I know what dad did was completely wrong, but he's still our dad. He's already apologized numerous times.

"Do you like it here?" He asked.

"Nope." I leaned against the counter in the center of the kitchen and crossed my arms over my chest. "I am the only black person at school, and the teachers are racist."

"Have you told your mother?"

I sighed. "No, I don't want to bother her with it. She's been really stressed lately with work and everything."

My dad smiled at me. "You are such a good kid Lizzy, don't let those kids at school bother you." I just nodded. It was going to be hard to ignore people.

I heard a loud thud and little footsteps running down the hallway. "Daddy!" McKenna jumped into dad's arms giggling. I decided to go up to my room to start my homework. I walked past Cameron's room and pounded on the door. There was loud music blasting.

"Come in." I heard him say.

I opened the door and he was laying on his bed staring at the ceiling. I walked over to his laptop and pressed pause on the media player. "What's the matter with you?"

"What are you talking about? I'm fine."

"You have to forgive dad sooner or later, you know." I said.

"I choose later." He finally sat up and looked at me. "Mom didn't deserve that. Nobody does." He said the last part quietly.

I pulled a strand of my naturally curly dark hair. "Give him a chance, he's trying."

"Yeah, I'll think about it." He quickly changed the subject. "I thought you were going to Taylor's house."

"Her step-mom is scary."

He laughed. "I'm going to the mall with Ben, Ryan, and Kevin later. Would you like to come?"

"Sure."

"You can bring Taylor, if you want." Cameron suggested.

"Okay" What harm could going to the mall bring?

Chapter 5

E rin maguire pictured above

I clutched my stomach tightly as Ben, Cameron, and I entered the mall. Where are Kevin, Ryan, and Taylor, you ask? Taylor's step mom would not let her out of the house; Kevin and Ryan, for now, are just lost causes. So I had to sit in a car with Ben driving. Let's just say, his driving isn't very safe, and I had never got car sick until now. I will never get in a car with him ever again, but Cameron sure seemed to enjoy the ride.

Cameron and Ben look at me and start cracking up. "You okay?" Ben asked.

I put on a fake smile. "Just trying to control the vomit rising in my throat." This made them laugh even harder. I really don't understand why guys find everything funny.

We entered the mall and it felt like I had stepped into a completely different universe. It was like several Barbie and Ken dolls had come to life. As people walked past me they glared. I really did fit in well here at all.

I then realized Cameron and Ben had absent mindedly went ahead and left me to stand there and soak in my surroundings. I quickly spotted them and I followed them into Hollister. That store always annoyed me for some reason. I was just wandering around, bored, and I noticed a lady who worked there had been kind of following me. Seriously, what am I gonna steal from Hollister?

"Welcome to Hollister. Can I help you with anything?" She asked.

I gave her a weird look. "Can I help YOU?"

"Excuse me?" She asked stupidly like I wasn't speaking plain English.

"You seem like the one who needs help." I said as I walked past her looking for Cameron and Ben.

"Can we leave now?" I asked once I finally found them. "This place is boring. And this creepy lady is stalking me."

"Yeah, we're leaving soon." Cameron said. In annoyance, I spun around on my heel and bummped right into the same lady who was following me. "Haven't you ever heard of personal space?"

"Well excuse you." She said looking down at me from head toe in disgust. "You are not wanted in this store any way."

"Oh really?" I pretend to sound hurt and crossed my arms over my chest. "If you really think I want to steal something, you are terribly mistaken. I HATE THIS STORE! WHY WOULD I TAKE ANYTHING?! Does this have to do with the fact that im black?"

The lady seemed taken aback by my words. "I-I.." She didn't know what to say.

I felt Cameron pulled my arm. "Liz, come on." He pleaded.

I whipped myself around in anger to face him. "Why do you keep doing this? Can't you ever stick up for me just once?"

"I do stick up for you!" Cameron argued. "Lizzy, can we just talk about this somewhere else?"

"Why can't we talk about it right now?" Then a sudden realization washed over me like an epiphany. I took a step back and looked at my so called brother very carefully. "I never thought you of all people would be embarassed of me, Cameron."

"That's not why--" Cameron began but I quickly cut him off.

"Of course it's not. I'll save you the embarrassment and leave. Just let me know when your done in here." I stormed out of Hollister without turning back. I wandered around in anger until I found a bench nearby to sit on. Cameron has never acted like this before. It's this whole place, I know it.

I pulled out my cellphone to check the time. I really just wanted to go back home, our real home back where we used to live. Out of the corner of my eye I saw somebody approach me. I looked up to see Ben standing in front of me.

"Hi." I said glumly while staring straight ahead.

"Hey." He sat down on the bench beside me. "Looking around isn't as fun without you. You keep Cameron and me entertained."

"I'm not entertaining." I said stifly still looking straight ahead.

"Lizzy," Ben said in a serious tone and I turned my head to look at him. "I'm really sorry about what happened in there. It's not right at all." He paused. "And now Cameron feels terrible and he's sorry."

"Then why couldn't he come tell me that himself?" I asked annoyed.

"Because you were mad at him."

"I still am!" I exclaimed. "You don't understand, nobody does. How would you feel if you were suddenly dragged to an all black town? How would you handle it?" The look on Ben's face told me that he was in deep thought. "Exactly." I said.

--

"The entire Junior class will be taking a camping trip." My homeroom teacher exclaimed. OH NO. No way hell was I going camping, especially in the woods where crazy animals could live.

I raised my hand. "When is this camping trip?"

"In two weeks." The teacher responded.

"Is it mandatory?"

"Yes, Lizzy, this trip is mandatory. It will count as a project grade in your science classes." Damn it. This is like forcing someone not to breath. It's inhumane. "Why me...why me.." I mumbled. I heard Ben snicker behind me. "Shut up." I said. In the past few days, his annoyance has spurred.

"I have assigned you all partners to stick with during the trip." The teacher said. I sighed. She started reading off our partners, when she got to my name she paused.

"Lizzy, you will be partnered up with Ben."

"Hell no!" Ben and I said in unison. I turned around and glared at him. I will get so annoyed with him.

"Well since the two of you apparently dislike each other, I think putting you two together will be a beneficial thing." She had a thoughtful look on her face. "Actually, I want everyone, after the trip, to tell the class something positive about your partner."

I groaned. My life just keeps getting worse by the minute.

--

Taylor had to stay after school so I had to walk home by myself, in the pouring rain, without a hood. Cameron, being the lucky one, got a ride from that biatch Erin.

I really shouldn't have straightened my hair this morning. I could see tight curls forming on the side of my face. I was walking near the curb when a car sped by, sending a huge puddle of water splattering all over me.

"FUCKKKK!" I yelled. Thunder boomed above me. If I get electrocuted by the lightening, this will officially be my worst day ever. I walked up my driveway drenched with water. My teeth were already chattering and I was shivering from the cold when I entered my house.

"What the hell happened to you? Cameron asked. Did he not see the water dropping from the sky? I ignored him and my eyes fell on Taylor sitting across from him in the living room.

"What are you doing here? I thought you stayed after school." I said shakily.

She had a sad look on her face for some reason. "Uh, Cameron, I need to talk to Lizzy...alone."

Cameron looked at me, I shrugged. He left and went upstairs. "Lizzy..I'm really glad we're friends, and –"

"Taylor, what exactly are you trying to say?" I cut her off.

"My step mother....she doesn't want me to be friends with you." She avoid-ed eye contact with me.

"Why?" I asked shocked. Taylor gave me a look, and I understood. "..Bec ause I'm black..."

Official worst day ever...confirmed.

Chapter 6

"You idiot, we already passed this tree two times." I groaned. Ben and I had been walking for at least an hour, and my feet already started hurting. Why couldn't this stupid camping trip be cancelled? It looked like it would rain soon, and here we were searching for a raggedy old green flag. How would we find it? We are in the woods and that's like trying to find someone dressed in camouflage.

"Do you think you could do any better reading this map?" Ben asked.

"Nope. I'd be better off with a GPS." I snatched the map from his hands and studied it. "What's up with all these arrows?" I said to myself. I looked around, and then looked at Ben. "Which way is north?"

He shrugged and pointed up. I rolled my eyes and sighed. "Why don't you make an educated guess?" He asked.

The directions all around us looked the same so I just picked one. "Okay, that's north. If it's not, which I highly doubt it is, don't blame me."

Ben and I began to walk "north". "We were supposed to be back at the camp thirty minutes ago." He looked at his watch. "We've been looking for this flag for an hour."

"Yeah, yeah, yeah." I mumbled and took out my cell phone. "There is no connection in this place!" I exclaimed. "What if we never find our way back? I'll be stuck with you!" I started to panic. I had to find a way back to the camp.

"You are getting paranoid. You are such a pessimist. " Ben said picking up his pace. "Who wouldn't want to be stuck in the woods with me?" He smirked.

"Such a big word for a small brain. Don't flatter yourself." I rolled my eyes. I don't even know where I'm going. "Can we stop for a minute?"

"Sure." Ben shrugged. We stopped and sat on a log. "I'm starving, man!" Ben shouted.

"Me too." Then I remembered mom packed me three sandwiches! I went digging through my backpack and I found it and held it front of my face like I just found a million dollars. "Mom you're the best!" I flung one at Ben and we both maxed on those sandwiches. I saved the last one just in case we got hungry later.

There were mosquitoes flying around my face and I tried swatting them away. "Stupid mosquitoes. Eww."

"I assume you aren't the outdoor type person." Ben laughed. I rolled my eyes.

Just then it started to drizzle. Too bad Taylor wasn't on this trip to share my misery. She hasn't been over my house in a while. We only talked at school, and I had to walk home by myself. I miss her boy crazed self sometimes.

I remembered when I first met her. Then out of nowhere I randomly started laughing just thinking about it.

"What?" Ben looked at me.

I shook my head. "Nothing, I wish I could talk to Taylor right now. I haven't laughed in a while."

"I don't understand what happened. Why can't she be friends with you anymore?" Ben asked.

"Because her step mother doesn't approve of my dark pigment." I said. "Apparently black people are bad examples. It's not even fair, Ben. It's not fair."

"I'm sorry, Lizzy." Ben said softly, and he actually sounded sympathetic. Then it started to rain harder, followed by a loud clap of thunder.

"Let's forget about the flag and try to find our way back." I said. Ben's curly dark hair was matted onto his head. We continued to walk and at about 3:15 in the afternoon the sun came up and the skies cleared.

"This weather is bipolar." Ben said, then he turned to me. "Do you think they've noticed we're lost yet?"

I laughed. "Nope. They will all be trying to remember that BLACK girl's name."

He laughed, then smirked. "They all will realize that handsome, cool guy is missing."

"Keep dreaming." I got bored from walking so I started to sing instead.

"Remember all the things we wanted

Now all our memories, they're haunted

We were always meant to say goodbye

Even with our fists held high

It never would have work out right, yeah

We were never meant for do or die

I didn't want us to burn out

I didn't come here to hurt you now I can't stop

I want you to know

That it doesn't matter

Where we take this road

But someone's gotta go

And I want you to know

You couldn't have loved me better

But I want you to move on

So I'm already gone—"

I stopped singing and turned to Ben. "My singing isn't disturbing you, is it?"

He smiled. "Not at all. Your voice is amazing. Why would it bother me?"

I shrugged remembering one of my foster moms. "Some people may not like to hear me sing."

"Whoever wouldn't want to hear you sing is just jealous." Ben looked at me and smirked. "Can I ask you a personal question?"

I eyed him suspiciously. "How personal?"

"It's nothing bad or anything.."

"What?" I asked annoyed.

"Is your hair real?"' He asked. I stopped abruptly and my mouth hung open. I cannot believe he just asked me that. Then I couldn't help but laugh and laugh until I couldn't stop.

Is this what goes through every non black person's head? If that black woman's hair is real or not? "Yes, believe it or not, it's my real hair." I said. "I got it from my birth mother, she had long hair." Ben stared at me in disbelief. "You can pull it if you want, it won't come out." I laughed and held out my hair for him to hold.

Ben gently tugged on my hair and was fascinated by it. "intersting.."

Oh Lord.

I burst out into hysterical laughter again. "That just made my day, Ben."

"I love your laugh, you have a beautiful smile." Oh goodness, that was such a nice compliment. My face would probably be red now.

Oh, the many advantages of being black.

I did not know how to respond to that so I quickly mumbled a, "Thank you."

We continued to walk in silence until Ben asked. "Is it okay if I ask you about your biological parents?"

I hated bringing it up, because I didn't like remembering. I decided it was better to talk about it then to keep it in. "Yeah, sure. Uh, well on my fifth birthday, my mother and father took me to Chuck E Cheese to celebrate. I remember that day so vividly; they got me this karaoke machine I wanted so badly, because I loved to sing. On the way back from celebrating my birthday we went on the expressway to get home faster." My voice cracked. I felt a lump in my throat.

"You..don't have to go on..if.." Ben said quietly.

"No, it's alright." I haven't cried in year, but I've gotten so used to telling this story that it's not as bad. I continued on. "There was a loud 'boom' and a sharp jolt from the impact of a semi truck colliding with our car. I heard my mother scream and my father hollered out my little brother's name, then mine, right before the car flipped right over into a ditch." I tried to shake out the mental picture, but it wouldn't go away.

"I was holding my brother, Jaden's hand. I knew he was scared, and I heard him cry, he was only two years old. " I choked out the last part. "I think lost consciousness after that, because the next thing I remember is waking up in a hospital. I was having pains in my chest...I crushed four of my ribs. A nurse came in and told me...she told me that..." I stopped talking. This was harder than I thought.

Ben looked down at me with sympathetic eyes. I hated knowing that people felt sorry for me. It made me angry almost. I never thought him of all people would have such empathy. "They didn't make it..." He said. I bit my lip and shook my head slowly. I heard Ben swear under his breath, "But Your brother was so young.."

"Jaden..he and I survived. Some family adopted him. ," I kicked a rock with my foot. "Life goes on." I said.

The sun was setting and we still had no idea where we were going; plus the ground was disgusting and muddy. "Can I ask you another question?"

"Yeah." I said, not caring whether it was personal or not.

"Are those real?" Ben said looking at me BELOW eye level I followed his gaze....to my boobs!

I gave him a hard shove. "You pervert. It's all natural, like the hair on my head!" He started laughing, and I did too.

"I'm sorry; most girls at school get implants, so I just wasn't sure." Ben said.

"I'm not like those girls."

Ben looked me in the EYE and said, "I know."

I rolled my eyes. "Come on Mr. Curiosity. I think we've both had enough interrogating for one day." I remembered Ben's question about my hair. "Atleast I have.." I started laughing again, and Ben looked at me and smiled.

I suddenly stopped laughing and grabbed Ben's arm to stop him from walking any further. I stared in horror at what was ahead of us. Ben followed my terrified gaze to the huge bear laying down a few feet in front of us. It looked to be asleep. Shouldn't they be hibernating or something right now?

"Stay calm, Lizzy." Ben whispered. CALM? A 600 POUND BEAR IS INCHES AWAY AND HE WANTS ME TO BE CALM?? Yeah, my ass. "Back up, slowly." He said.

We both took large steps away from the bear, not taking our eyes off of it. I stepped on a twig, and it snapped in half sounding like a piercing gunshot.

Just then the bear's eyes shot open and it stood on its hind legs and growled.

This bear is going to eat us alive.

Chapter 7

I jumped back, surprised and how huge the bear was. I've never been so scared in my life. It stared at Ben and me and moved closer. A weird noise escaped my throat, and I moved backwards.

"Don't move." Ben whispered. Then he suddenly started talking to the freakin bear, as if it understood English!

"We're leaving now. We are not going to hurt you." Ben's voice was soft. It actually worked. The bear settled back onto the ground, seeming calmer than before. "Alright, now back up carefully." He said to me.

He didn't have to tell me twice. As soon as we were out of the bear's sight, I began to run for my life, hoping to put as much distance away from me and that beast.

"Lizzy, slow down!" I heard Ben shout. I stopped running and turned to see Ben jogging towards me. "What is your problem?"

"That bear was going to KILL us. How did you do that?" I asked.

He smirked. "I used to be a boy scout." His eyes averted to my leg. "Oh, you're bleeding." I looked down at my leg and there was a deep cut across my shin.

"It was probably a sharp twig, it's no big deal."

Ben had a concerned expression on his face. "You don't want it to get infected." He motioned for me to sit on the log nearby. He rummaged through his backpack and took out the first-aid kit the teachers gave us.

Ben patted his lap for me to lift my leg up. I was hesitant, because it was a little awkward, but I did anyway. He took out the hydrogen peroxide and poured some onto the cut and it foamed. It started to sting really badly. I bit my lip to fight the pain.

He looked at me. "Does it hurt?"

WHAT THE HELL DO YOU THINK? I let out a nervous laugh. "Just a little."

"I'm sorry. " He touched my leg, and I jumped, startled by his soft touch. He laughed. "You're a little jumpy, aren't you."

I laughed nervously again. WHAT IS WRONG WITH ME? "No, I'm not."

Ben smirked. "You were scared. Weren't you?"

"I was not that scared!" I lied. "You were probably scared."

"Fine, don't admit it, but I know you were." He said. After Ben cleaned up my leg, he wrapped gauze around it. His touch made me feel, different, in some weird way I can't explain.

"You are really good at this." I complimented.

"I should be if I want to be a surgeon." He said.

"YOU?" I was astonished. "You want to be a surgeon?"

He laughed. "Is that so hard to believe?"

"um, yeah!" I said. When he finished tending to my injury, he gently placed my leg back on the ground. "Thanks."

"No problem."

I looked around. "Uh-oh. It's getting dark." Ever since I was young, I hated the dark. I still even have to sleep with a lamp on. It's always scared me.

"We might as well just sleep out here."

"NO! No, we can't sleep out here." I was starting to panic. "It's not safe." Just then we heard a howling sound in the distance. My eyes widened. "There are wolves out here?"

Ben chuckled and I looked at him and realized I was clinging to his arm tightly. I moved away quickly. "Sorry." I mumbled.

"Don't be scared, we'll be fine." Ben said trying to sound reassuring, but failed. "I won't let anything happen to us."

I wonder what Cameron's doing right now. I bet he's sitting around a warm campfire laughing, or in a tent sleeping, or worse, making out with Erin Maguire. "That bitch." I thought out loud.

Ben gave me a weird look. "What and who are you talking about?"

"Erin Maguire."

"Oh, THAT bitch." He probably has heard this before. "I still can't believe I went out with her. She still wants to be with me, but I just don't have feelings for her." Ben looked at me. "I'm sorry to say this, Lizzy, but I'm pretty sure she's getting close to Cameron to make me jealous."

"Why are you saying sorry to me? You should inform Cameron since he's such an airhead. " I would tell Cameron, but he wouldn't listen to me anyway. "I miss my sister." I said randomly.

"I miss my parents." Ben said.

"I need to meet them some time."

"IF ,we ever find our way back." He said in a serious tone. I gave him a blank stare, and he laughed. "I'm only kidding." I rolled my eyes, and felt around my pocket for my cell phone. I took it out and I still had no signal. I yawned. I was tired and sleepy from this long exhausting trip.

I wish I was in my warm cozy bed listening to my ipod. The air around me suddenly got colder and I started to shiver. I looked down at my arms and they were covered with goosebumps. Why does my life keep getting complicated? First, I move to a place where I'm not even—

My thoughts were interrupted by Ben's light snoring next to me. His head was leaned against a tree trunk, sound asleep. HOW CAN HE SLEEP WHEN WE ARE STRANDED IN THE FOREST?! Now I'm practically alone now. I looked at the darkness around me, and then at Ben.

So much for not letting anything happen to us. I sighed in frustration.

Suddenly I heard heavy footsteps in the distance. My heart started beating fast. I shook Ben frantically. "Ben! Wake up!" I whispered.

"Hmmm?" He mumbled and opened his eyes. "What, Lizzy?"

"I think there's someone coming."

He rubbed his eyes, stood up and turned on his flashlight and we both listened. "I don't hear anything."

"Lizzy! Ben!Where are you?!" I heard familiar voice call out in the distance. Ben and I exchanged a curious glance. We both definitely heard our names being called.

"Who's there?" Ben shouted.

"Ben?! Can you guys follow the sound of my voice" The familiar voice said.

We grabbed our backpacks, and Ben gently took my hand so we wouldn't be separated in the darkness. We listened for the soft footsteps up ahead and Cameron appeared infront of us.

I ran to him as fast as I could and wrapped my arms around him, nearly knocking him over. "Cameron! I thought I'd never see you again!" He laughed. I've never missed my brother so much.

"I thought you guys were dead, or something." Cameron said almost too casually. "I got really scared so I came out looking for you guys." He looked down at my leg and his eyes went wide. "What happened to you? Are you okay?"

"Yeah, I'm fine. Just cut myself." I said.

"We almost died encountering a bear." Ben said and looked at me. "Lizzy was scared as hell." They both started laughing. They always laugh at me!

"Shut up." I snapped.

"I can't wait to tell mom." Cameron said. I rolled my eyes.

"Do you know your way back?" I asked, and Cameron nodded. "How?"

He showed me a compass in his hand. "The staff gave each pair a compass." I gave him a confused look. "If I didn't have the compass, that means..." I glared at Ben.

He smiled nervously. "Oh, I thought that was some foreign clock, or something." He pulled a compass out of his backpack.

I slapped my forehead in frustration. I could have not been lost out here for several hours if this idiot knew what a compass was. Ben tried to say something, but I stopped him. "Please, don't speak." I said.

On the way back, we passed by a tree with a green flag tied around it. I felt like I needed a stress ball at the moment. We followed Cameron for while until we got back to camp. "I think everyone went to sleep." Cameron said.

I feel so loved. "Did the teacher's plan on looking for us anytime soon?" I asked.

"Tomorrow morning." Cameron said. We could have been dead by then. I groaned, it was twelve o' clock midnight. I had to wait another 24 hours before I'd get to go home. "Eff my life." I yawned and went into my designated tent and fell into a deep sleep.

It felt like I only slept for twenty minutes instead of five hours. It was six in the morning and the sun was beginning to rise. The teachers thought it was the perfect time to wake up a bunch of teenager and force them to go fishing.

They wanted to see which pair could catch the most fish in an hour. FUNNNN! Yeah..no.

"Are you gonna get off your ass and do something." Ben said while trying to catch some fish. While, I, being very resourceful took the opportunity to take a nap.

"I am doing something." I retorted. "I'm looking out for lions, and tigers, and bears, oh my" I whispered the last part.

"With your eyes closed?"

"I can sense these things, okay?" I lied. "Give me a break, I'm tired and I'm not the mood to do this."

Ben tossed the fishing poles aside and sat next to me. "It's not like I got enough sleep either."

"It was your fault we got lost for like 9 hours yesterday in the first place!" I rolled my eyes. "Why would we be given a foreign clock? If you had common sense then I wouldn't be as pissed as I am now!" I was really grouchy when it was this early.

"You can't blame me for this!" Ben said defensively. "It was an honest mistake."

"Give me one good reason why you are not to blame for my troubles, Ben." I said fidgeting with the fishing pole next to me.

"Because I didn't let us get attacked by that bear." Ben said. Dang, He made a good point, but i wasn't going to give him the benefit of the doubt.

"I could have done the same..have a conversation with a bear." I said and Ben just laughed, even though i was completely serious. We sat in silence for a brief moment until Ben said five words i NOW hate hearing from him.

"Can I ask you something?" He said.

"Uh-oh..." I mumbled as I took my water bottle out of my backpack. "If this has anything to do with legit or false body parts..I'm gonna.."

He laughed. "Relax, it's a serious question." Ben paused. "Have you ever been in a relationship before?"

I took a drink from my water bottle. I hesitated for a moment. "Not exactly."

"Yes or no?"

"No. I haven't actually been in a true relationship." I said. "Why do you ask?"

"You haven't talked about your past life, so I was just curious." He shrugged.

Was he joking? I looked at him wide eyed. "I just told like half of my life story yesterday!"

"You didn't mention anything after you..." He looked nervous. "You kno w..."

"My parents died?" I asked plainly.

"Don't say it like that." He said.

"Really, it's okay." I looked down at started poking the ground with the fishing pole. "I'm not emotionally unstable. I just sometimes have dreams, and they're like these flashbacks of the accident." I felt Ben looking at me and then he put his hand over mine and squeezed it gently. "But other than that, i'm fine. See.." I stood up quickly and the stupid fishing pole hit my injured leg.

"OwWwWwWw!" I screeched, while hopping up and down like a maniac on one leg holding the other in pain.

Ben started laughing like crazy. " you are very clumsy, but very entertaining."

"Am I really THAT funny?"

"Yes."

"How?"

"Can I ask you a question?" Ben said.

I stopped hopping. "What the hell is wrong with you? Why do you ask so many fucking questions?" I asked ,and Ben started hysterically laughing again.

"See. I just wanted to see what you would do if I said that again." Ben stood up and stretched. I rolled my eyes.

Then I remembered something we had to do and I groaned. "I forgot about the whole 'writing something positive about your partner' from this experience." I glared at Ben. "You better not say anything insulting, or else I'll hurt you."

He smiled. "I can't even think of a single negative thing about you."

--

Finally! I was home in my warm bed and i was exhausted. It was the following morning, a monday, and we didn't have school because of some reason I'm unaware of but couldn't care less. I survived that camping trip being stuck with Ben, even though he wasn't as bad as I thought he would be. I can't believe I'm saying this, but he's actually a decent human being.

I woke up to the smell of blueberry pancakes. I sat up in my bed and looked around completely confused. Today wasn't anyone's birthday,it's not a holiday nad none of us had a friend sleep over. Mom only makes pancakes on a rare occasion, something was definitely wrong. I glanced the digital clock on my night stand. It was 11:08.

I rubbed my eyes and decided to take a shower. When I finished I slipped on a pair of jeans and a pink shirt. As I made my way downstairs I could hear mom singing, which is so unlike her.

"Good morning, honey." She said when she saw me. She was so cheery and smiley today.

Cameron and Mckenna were sitting at the table and it looked like they had just begun eating. I smiled. "Good morning, mom."

"I'll get you some pancakes." She then had her back to me and I gave Cameron a look and pointed at mom with a questioning look. He just shrugged and mouthed 'ask'. I pointed at him and said. "You ask."

Mom turned around, "What?"

I smiled. "Nothing." She handed me a plate with two blueberry pancakes. "Thanks, mom." I sat down across from Cameron.

"She's been like this all morning." He whispered. "I don't know what's going on."

I cut my pancakes with the side of my fork and brought a piece to my mouth. Mom started to hum now, and I looked at her. "She's glowing, Cameron." I said to him.

"What are you guys talking about." Mckenna whispered next to me.

"Nothing, mind your own business." Cameron said and I laughed.

Mckenna frowned. "Meanies."

"Mom..." I said.

"Yes?" She asked.

"What's wrong...with you?" I asked awkwardly, then i reprased the question. "I mean, why are you so happy today?"

She turned around and look at Mckenna, Cameron, and me and smiled. "Hmm..I guess I can tell you guys now.." I was confused.

"Tell us what?" Cameron asked.

Mom sighed. "I met this really great guy, his name is Luke." My jaw dropped in surprise and I glanced over at Cameron and he looked like someone had just slapped him across the face. "I didn't know when the right time was to tell you guys." She continued.

"Wow." Was all I could say. I was more shocked about the fact that mom was dating again. No wonder she was glowing like a candle.

"I think we should meet this guy." Cameron said. "Don't we Lizzy?"

"Yeah, of course." I said.

"Well, he's coming over for dinner tomorrow." Mom explained, she really didn't waste time. "He's a good man, and he makes me feel happy." I smiled, because she deserved to be happy. I looked at Mckenna and her expression had confusion written all over it.

Cameron looked at me and I knew what he was thinking. We were give 'Luke' a harsh interrogation. If mom's gonna date him, he has to be approved by us first.

He put on a fake smile. "Can't wait to meet him."

Chapter 8

"Please." I begged.

"No." Ben said flatly.

We were in homeroom and since we were running out of time the teacher told us to write down a POSITIVE paragraph about our camping partner instead of presenting it to the class. THANK GOODNESS. I was dying to see what Ben wrote about me, but he wouldn't let me have a glance at his paper. I was turned around in my seat and was trying to grab his paper off his desk, but he had his arm covering it.

"Why don't you want me to see it?" I asked, not taking my eyes off his paper.

"Because I don't."

I rolled my eyes. Why did Ben have to be so difficult. "Pleaseeee." I said in a sing song voice.

He smirked and shook his head. "You really don't take 'no' for an answer." His expression turned serious. "You really want to see what I wrote?" I nodded desperately and Ben smiled. "Too bad."

"Jerk." I turned around in my seat and looked down at my finished paragraph. It had nice things about Ben, mainly because we couldn't write anything bad. Then I had a brilliant idea! The teacher always asks us to pass forward our work and so since Ben sits behind me, I can read his paper.

Two minutes later the teacher asked us to pass up the assignment, Instead of passing it to me, Ben got up from his seat and walked all the way to the teacher to give it to her. UNBELIEVEABLE! He smirked at me when he walked by and I saw a glimpse of what he wrote on his paper in his hand. I leaned over in my chair to get a closer look, but I leaned to far and fell out of my chair onto the floor.

I heard a few people laugh, but I didn't care, because what I saw on that paper made me smile. As Ben came walking back to his seat he looked at me like I was crazy since I was sitting in the middle of the aisle.

"What are you doing on the floor?" He asked. "And why are you smiling?"

I automatically frowned after I realized I was smiling like an idiot and sat back in my seat. "No reason."

Then I instantly remembered those four words I managed to see: SHE GIVES ME HOPE. I never thought Ben was capable of putting those words in the same sentence. That was one of the nicest things anyone has said about me in a long time, and it made me feel good about myself.

--

Taylor disregarded her step mom's request and walked home with me that day after school. I told her about my fascinating time camping and how mom's new boyfriend, Luke, was coming over for dinner.

As we walked up the driveway Taylor asked, "Is Cameron home?"

"I think so, why?" I asked.

"Ooooh, yes!" She squealed. I rolled my eyes and pulled open the front door. There were loud noises coming from the living room. Taylor and I walked into the living room, and Cameron, Ben, and this one kid who came here before, but I forgot his name, were in there.

Anyway, they were playing rock band. Cameron was playing the guitar, Ben was playing the drums , and mystery boy was attempting to sing. We stood there and watched them until the song finished playing.

"Dude, you seriously suck at singing, Ryan." Ben said to the mystery kid whose name I just figured out was Ryan.

"Yeah, Lizzy would totally whoop your ass in singing." Cameron said and looked at me. "Right?" I just shrugged. He smiled Taylor and said, "Hey Taylor, I haven't seen you around in a while."

Taylor blushed and smiled idiotically, similar to what I did earlier. "Yeahh." Was all she said then she whispered in my ear. "He noticed I haven't been around! And he smiled at me!" I shook my head and laughed.

"Can I just tell him that you like him?" I asked.

Taylor shook her head. "I'll let him know, when the time is right." She looked at Cameron. "I don't even have courage to speak to him."

I pushed her closer to the three boys and said. "Taylor has never played Rock Band before. Can you teach her?"

"Sure..which one do you...?" I cut Cameron off.

"She wants to learn the guitar part." I said quickly, and they all gave me a strange look.

Cameron took the guitar thing off and handed it to Taylor, and she let out a nervous laugh. Ben picked a song and Cameron tried to explain what Taylor was suppose to do. "So when the blue comes up you press the blue button and press this down." He pointed. "When theres a long note you hold it down."

Taylor played dumb pretty well, atleast I thought she was pretending, but who knows. She missed the past ten notes and Cameron had to help to her press down the buttons. Her face was flaming red. I don't understand how Cameron doesn't notice that Taylor is like in love with him. Its so obvious.

I felt my phone vibrate in my pocket. I took it out and I got a text messege from Ben. I looked up at him and he was looking at me, waiting for me to read it.

it said: "There is a website I found that can help find your biological brother."

I looked at him wide eyed and he smiled. I grabbed his arm and dragged him up to my room, pushed him to my desk and stood in front of him with my arms crossed. "Explain."

"Okay, i heard about this amazing website that helps locate people." He said.

I stared at him then asked ,"How do you know for sure if that website is legit?"

"One of my cousins was adopted and he used it to find his birth parents. And it worked." Ben typed in the web address and the page came up. A feeling of dread came upon me and I sighed. "What's the matter?" Ben asked.

I ran my fingers through my thick brown hair. "I don't know his last name, though."

"That's fine, you can use your old last name." He said and waited for me to say something. "You forgot it?"

I scratched my head. "No, uh...crap..it's." It was right at the tip of my tongue. I think I had it somewhere. I went to my nightstand and looked through the drawers. They were filled with old papers and then i found it.

An old certificate for having perfect attendence to Sunday School. It said ELIZABETH RICHARDSON. I brought back with me to my desk. "Richardson." I told Ben and he typed Jaden Richardson.

About fifty names came up. He scrolled down and stopped at JADEN RICHARDSON (JADEN DONIVAN) "I think this is probably him, because he has two different last names." Ben said and I nodded. He clicked the link and Jaden's information appeared on the screen.

Name: Jaden Donivan

Age: 13

City: Wentworth

Occupation: Junior High School student

Wentworth was the town Jaden and I were born in. I did the math in my head and he would be thirteen years old today. There was an address and phone number and I copied them onto a sheet of paper.

"Thanks Ben, I owe you." I said.

Seeing that information just added on to my happy day. Then I had a sudden realization that both incidents had involved Ben. I wasn't sure if that was a good or bad thing. Either way, I was happy.

--

Three hours later, after Ben, Taylor, and Ryan left, the doorbell rang. It was Luke, and I put on a pink, knee high dress. It wasn't too dressy, but not too casual. Since it was his first time meeting us, mom wanted us to look nice to make a good first impression.

I was brushing my hair and I heard mom call me. "Lizzy! Luke's here!"

"Coming!" I shouted. I quickly made my way downstairs when I got to the dining room Mckenna and Cameron were seated with a middle aged man with light brown and a few wrinkles under his eyes sat at the table with a glass of water in hand. He looked up and when he saw me he instantly froze. The glass slipped out of his hand and broke into pieces on the floor.

The first thing that came to my mind was how uncoordinated this guy was. Then I thought about his reaction and assumed mom must not have described me very well.

"Oh I'm sorry!" Luke exclaimed. He looked up at me. "Miss, can you come clean this up?"He pointed down at his glass mess. Who was he talking to? I crossed my arms over my chest and stared at him.

My mother stood by his side and glanced at me nervously. She quickly told Luke to come with her into the kitchen. I went over by kitchen, but stayed out of sight so I could hear what they were saying.

"Your maid does not listen." Luke said and I was completely offended beyond belief.

My mom's eyes widened. "She is not our maid, Luke! She is my daughter Lizzy! I've already told you I adopted."

"But you didn't tell me she was....she was...black." Luke said.

"Why does that matter? Does it really matter to you?" Mom asked. I didn't want to hear his answer so I walked to the table and sat far away from Luke's seat as possible. Cameron was sweeping up the glass and I sat down at the table pissed.

"What an asshole." Cameron said to me. "He's so stupid." I didn't reply because my happy day was ruined. Mom can not date him. I already hate him. Cameron could ask Luke all the questions he wanted because he failed and I haven't even spoken a word to him yet.

Then Luke came trotting back into the room as if everything was all good, and mom followed behind him. He stood beside me, but I didn't bother to look up. "Elizabeth..."

"It's Lizzy. L-I-Z-Z-Y. Lizzy.." I spelled it out for him and said my name slowly so it would get through his ignorant head.

"I'm sorry....Lizzy, it's nice to meet you. I'm Luke." He said. At that point I didn't care if he was the king of England.

"Good to know." I said. I turned to my mom. "Can we eat now?"

"Yes! Let's eat!" Mom said and I helped put the food on the table. We were all seated at the table and mom said to me, "Lizzy, will you say grace?"

"Sure." I folded my hands together and so did everyone else except Luke. "You're not excluded." I said to him and he looked around the table nervously then folded his hands. I took a deep breath, closed my eyes, and prayed:

"Heavenly Father, we thank you for this beautiful day you created, for giving us the opportunity to gather here this evening. Please bless this meal we are about to partake..." I opened my eyes slightly and looked over at Luke. "And please heal the sick, and assist the cold-hearted, selfish, ignorant, rude, disrespectful, foo---"

"Amen!" Mom said interrupting into my prayer, and everyone repeated it also. I guess I was getting carried away, but can you blame me?

Dinner was..tedious, until Cameron started interrogating Luke. "What are your intentions with our mother?"

Luke restraightened his tie, "Well, I want to make her happy.She's a beautiful, intelligent woman who deserves to be loved." I rolled my eyes because I didn't want to hear any b.s.

"Are you willing to make her children happy?" Cameron asked connivingly, and Luke nodded. Cameron turned his attention to me. "Do you have any questions, Lizzy?"

I stared at Luke. "When's the last time you were checked for any sexually transmitted diseases?" I asked with a blank expression.

Mom began to cough. "Lizzy!" She exclaimed.

I shrugged. "It's a serious quesion." I looked back at Luke. "Are you going to answer my question?"

"I plead the fifth." He said.

That was the worse answer you could possibly give to that question.

I made a buzzing noise and fake smiled. "You failed, sir."

Chapter 9

After dinner with Luke I went up to my room to finish my homework. Mom and Luke were downstairs watching a movie, and I was definitely not going down there since I loathed him with a passion.

I changed out of my dress into more comfortable clothes. I sat at my desk and my laptop was still open to that website Ben showed me. I wasn't sure when I would call, or what I would say. Then I began thinking the worst. What if it isn't a good idea to see him.

Just as I was gathering my delicate thoughts, my bedroom door swung open and Cameron walked in. I instantly shut my laptop so he would not see what was on the screen. He stood and stared at me for a moment.

"Do you need something?" I asked impatiently.

"Why'd you close your laptop?" He eyed me suspiciously.

"Why not?" I retorted.

Cameron came closer. "You're hiding something, aren't you?"

"No...I'm...I'm not hiding anything." I'm awful at lying so I avoided looking at him. I sighed, because Cameron could read me better than anyone else could. "You promise not to tell mom..yet."

He stood beside me, leaning back against my desk facing me. "This must be good."

I rolled my eyes and told Cameron about what Ben showed me, and how I found Jaden. Throughout my entire explanation, Cameron's expression showed me he was dissecting each word that came out of my mouth. Then he finally said, "Alright, my mind is offically blown."

I nodded and opened my laptop and showed the information to Cameron. "It has everything right here."

"Are you gonna go see him?" Cameron asked.

I bit my bottom lip. "Well, I would like to, but..." I trailed off.

"But...?" He egged on.

"I'm too freaked out to call. What if he's mad and thinks that I left him." i thought of something horrible and looked at Cameron wide eyed. "Or worse, what if he has no memory of me or any idea who I am!"

Cameron put a comforting hand on my shoulder "Lizzy, calm down. I'm sure he knows who you are. I know I haven't exprienced all that you've gone through, but when you decide to call..let me know. I'll be there. You know, for moral support." He gave me a reassuring smile.

I smiled. "Aw thanks thats probably that nicest thing you've said to me."

He frowned. "I've said many nice things to you."

I scoffed. "Like what?"

Cameron paused. "When I think of them, I'll tell you."

I laughed. "Okay, sure." I fidgeted with a pencil on my desk and began to tap it. "When should I tell mom?"

"Anytime. I think she'll be cool with it." Cameron started heading for my door and said, "You should start your homework. Don't worry about it too much." I just nodded even though I was going to continue worrying.

Before Cameron reached my door her turned to me and said, "You know even though you found your biological brother...I'm still gonna be your brother no matter what. I don't care if blood is thicker than water." He walked out of my room and gently closed the door before I could even respond.

Was he being sincere or was that jealously I sensed? I shrugged it off and went back to the drawer beneath my nightstand. I took out the family picture of me when I was five, jaden was two, and both my parents. It was months before the accident. I lightly moved my thumb over Jaden's small face.

Picturing him at age thirteen was strange. Then my gaze went to my mom. I resembled her so much. She was so beautiful.

"I miss you guys...and I love you.." I said.

--

In my dream I saw my biological mother. We were in a car and daddy was driving. My mother was turned in her seat, saying something to me I couldn't quite make out. I looked at my brother who was sitting beside me in his carseat. He was staring out the window sucking his thumb.

Then I heard a loud noise from behind, and glass shattering.

"Lizzy!" My mother said. "Jaden!"

The car skidded off the roadway and turned over.

I still kept hearing the voice. "Lizzy! Lizzy! Lizzzzzzyyyyy"

I opened my eyes and I was sitting at my desk in Calculus. My teacher, Mrs. Pike, was glaring down at me. I didn't get much sleep last night. Mostly because I kept thinking about Jaden.

"Wow, you are a deep sleeper." She said. "I've been trying to wake you up for the past minute." I looked around and everybody else was staring at me. I groaned and put my head back on my desk, because I wanted to continue sleeping.

"Sorry." I mumbled without any emotion.

"You look a little frightened. What were you dreaming about?" She asked. People should really mind their own business.

"Death." I said just to freak Mrs. Pike out, and everybody stared at me like I was crazy. I noticed Ben sitting up front, turned with his eyes wide. Then I started laughing.

The teacher frowned. "I don't know whether I should send you to the dean or a therapist." I held in my laugh while she contemplated. She tapped her foot and said, "Go to the dean."

"Okay." I said happily to get out of that class.

I walked slowly to the deans office. The dean was a tall, well built guy with few wrinkles and brown hair. He sat at his desk anxiously waiting for troublesome kids to get sent down. When I entered he looked at me and instantly shook his head in disapproval.

"Have a seat." He motioned for me to sit down in the chair acrosss from him. I sat and stared at him blankly. "Didn't you just move here a few weeks ago?" I nodded slowly. "Yes, I remember." Mostly because I stick out like a sore thumb here. He continued, "What brings you here?"

"I fell asleep in Mrs. Pike's class. Sue me why don't you." I said.

He raised his eyebrows. "Well what does she expect me to do for you? Give you coffee and send you back to class?" He asked in annoyance and I laughed.

"I have no idea. I think she just hates teaching."

The dean pulled open file cabinet full of manilla folders. "Your last name is West right."

"Yes."

He began looking through, "Elizabeth West." He said outloud as he came across my name and pulled out a folder and opened it. "Well you have a clean record, the only thing in here is your transcript and you've had mostly A's so far so there's not much I can tell you."

"I guess I'll try not to fall asleep in class." I ran my index finger across the desk and flicked the dust off. The bell rang, signaling the end of the period. Sounds filled the hallways as students walked by.

"Alright, you can go to your next class, and I will tell Mrs. Pike that you agreed not to fall asleep anymore. Is that a deal?" He asked, but I didn't understand how it was a deal if thats exactly what I was gonna do in the first place.

I just nodded and forced a smile. "Okay, thanks." I stood up and took a deep breath, which made my chest ache. The next period was my lunch period so I made my way to the cafeteria. The bell had already rung and there was barely anybody walking the halls.

In the distance I saw a guy and a girl standing very close together. The girl had her back against the lockers and the guy was leaning down towards her, shoving his tongue in her mouth. When I got close enough I saw that it was Cameron and Erin.

"Um. Ew." I said loudly. They both stopped to look my way. "That's pretty disgusting."

"Oh, Hey..Liz." Cameron said hesistantly as if he had been caught stealing something.

"Thanks for interrupting us." Erin said nastliy.

I forced a fake smile. "Oh, it was my pleasure." I walked past them, but Cameron stopped me.

"Hey, wait, I heard you got sent to the dean's office. What happened?" He asked.

I slowly jerked my arm away. "Nothing really. I just hacked into Ms. Pike's computer and changed my grade." I said sarcastically.

"Woah seriously? I always knew you were a genius." Cameron leaned close to me , "Do you think you could change my grade in physics, im almost failing."

I rolled my eyes and laughed. "I was kidding. I just dozed off in..."

"Hellooo. Cameron!" Erin said angrily, "Did you forget about me?" She had her arms crossed over chest with an annoyed expression on her face.

"I'll see you later, Cameron." I said and walked towards the cafeteria. I headed down the hallway and turned a corner and bumped into somebody. I realized I had ran into Ben. The books I had been carrying collided with his books and pushed heavily against my chest and fell to the floor.

"I am so sorry Lizzy." Ben said as he bent down to pick up the books. I couldn't even move, my chest ached so badly. "Are you okay?"

"Oh, I'm fine." I said trying to take slow breaths so Ben wouldn't know how much pain I was feeling. Ben stood back up and handed me my books.

"Did I hurt you? I'm so sorry." He apologized again with worried features on his face.

"Really, I'm okay." I forced a laugh. That was a bad idea because it made the pain much worse, and I grimaced.

Ben took my books out of my hands. "No. where does it hurt?" It was nice to know that he actually cared.

"You're crazy. Nothing hurts." I retrieved my books from him. "It was my fault too, sorry." When Ben didn't say anything I quickly changed the subject. "Where are you going? Shouldn't you be in lunch?"

"I was going to put these books in my locker." He explained. "Have you seen Cameron?"

"Oh, yeah, he's around the corner tongue wrestling with Erin." I said. The pain in my chest subsided.

"That's not something I want to see." Ben said shaking his head.

"Too bad I'm still scarred."

--

Later that day when I went home, I managed to tell my mom about Jaden. Her reaction surprised me, because she said, "Oh Lizzy, thats wonderful!" She was jumping happily in the kitchen. "Have you called him yet?" She asked.

"No."

"Well go ahead and call." She wrapped her arms around me and hugged me. "I'm so happy for you..and I'm so proud of you." Mom let go of me and pushed towards the hallway. "Go call..now."

I laughed and said, "Okay." I jogged up the stairs to my room and found the phone number. I took my cell phone out of my pocket and remembered Cameron was supposed to be with me.

I went to knock on Cameron's door, but there was loud Eminem music playing. Instead I just opened the door, and Ben was sitting against the wall with his Anatomy book open. Cameron was sitting at his desk in front of his laptop.

"Oh." I said, unaware that Ben was with him.

"Hey." Ben said.

"Hey." I said.

Cameron turned down the music and stared at me. "Well...?"

I waved my cell phone in the air. "I was going to call now.." I looked back and forth between Cameron and Ben. "But if you're busy.." I started walking out.

"No, I'm not." Cameron said.

"Who are you calling?" Ben asked.

"My brother." I said.

"I want to hear this, too." He said. I sat on the edge of Cameron's unmade bed.

"You two better not say ANYTHING." I stressed the last word and looked at Cameron and Ben. "Is that clear?" And they both nodded. I dialed the number and put my phone on speaker.

After two rings a woman answered the phone. "Hello?"

I froze and my heart began to beat rapidly.

"Hello?" The woman repeated, but I still couldn't speak.

Her voice sounded exactly like..my mother who was supposed to be dead.
She did die.....didn't she?

Chapter 10

"Uhhh.." I couldn't think of anything to do, but immediately end the call.

"What'd you do that for!" Cameron exclaimed. I jumped to my feet and began to pace back and forth in his room. "Lizzy, you hung up on her!"

I rolled my eyes. "Really? I wasn't aware." I said sarcastically to Cameron's dumb statement. "Her voice...she sounded like my mother.." I said quietly.

"What?!" Cameron and Ben said in unison, which made my head throb in pain.

"Are you sure?" Ben asked.

I rubbed my temples with my index and middle fingers. "I don't know, maybe I was hearing things, but I remember my birth mother's voice, and that woman sounded exactly like her."

"Maybe it was her." Cameron said stupidly, and I just ignored him. I continued to pace while Cameron was still talking to me.

I waved my hand in the air. "Shh!" I was trying to think of what to do now.

"Lizzy, that means your mother may be alive." Cameron said.

I froze and stared at Cameron and Ben in shock as I pondered on those words. "Thats...impossible. I went to the funeral..." I tried to remember that second horrible day in my life.

Everyone stood up and walked out of the rows of pews. The woman from child services, Miss Jordan, motioned for me to stand also. I did as I was told and smoothed out my black dress. The people formed a line walking past the two caskets laid out up front.

I recognized a few faces, like my mom and dad's close friends. Miss Jordan held my hand as we stood in line. As we neared the caskets I began to cry. It was like a horrible nightmare, except for the fact that it was completely real.

I touched my mothers lifeless hand, and it felt cold. "Mommy!" I exclaimed. "Please Mommy.." I looked and my father. "Daddy!"

Miss Jordan pulled me away gently. "Come on Sweetie." She took a tissue and wiped the tears off my face, but it was no use. The tears kept flowing out of my eyes.

Just standing here in Cameron's room thinking about it made me want to cry, but I held back my tears.

I looked at Cameron and Ben with a serious expresssion. "Trust me...she's not alive." I said and that shut Cameron up pretty fast. I don't think I'll be calling back anytime soon. The only thing that I didn't understand was why that woman's voice sounded so similar to my mother's.

Just then my phone my phone started playing "Find your love" by Drake. I walked quickly over to Cameron's bed where I left it and looked at who was calling.

"It's her!" I hissed frantically. I looked at Cameron and Ben in panic.

"I'll talk to her." Ben said , and I tossed him my phone across the room. "Hello?" He answered. Cameron and I watched Ben intently. "Yes, my name is Bob..uh Johnson, and I was calling on behalf of Jaden Donivan. Is he your son?" Ben waited for the woman to reply, then said. "Well, I am part of a...uh..a locating company within the state, and would like to inform you that Elizabeth West claims that she is Jaden's biological sister. Are you aware that he has a sister?" Ben asked, and looked at me, smiled and gave me a thumbs up telling me that she knows of my existence.

"Yes, that would be great." He said and made a scribbling action in the air with his hand. I quickly grabbed a pen from a desk nearby, and Cameron slid him his notebook.

Ben scribbling down some information. "Yes. Yes, I will be sure to tell her. Thank you so much for your time. Goodbye." He slid my phone shut. Who knew Ben Campbell was a genius?

"Well....?" I asked curiously.

"Let's just say, you'll be seeing Jaden in two weeks." Ben said and smiled.

"Once again, I owe you. Thank you so so much." I said to Ben.

Mckenna skipped happily into the room, "Daddy's here! And he bought Cameron a new car!"

"No effing way!" I exclaimed, and all of us rushed downstairs, and out the front door to the driveway and there was a silver BMW which didn't belong to Dad.

"Woah!" Ben exclaimed and went to touch the car. What is it with boys and cars?

"Don't you think this is a bit much?" Mom asked concerned.

"You seriously got this for him?!" I asked.

He nodded and said, "Surprise Cameron! Since you had to sell your old car before the move, I decided to give your driving privileges back with your own car."

Cameron just stared at the car in silence like it was some 1990 station wagon, and not a BMW. WAS HE FREAKING INSANE?!

"Dad, if Cameron doesn't want it, can I have it? Please, please." I begged.

"Lizzy." Mom gave me an 'of course you can't' look "Go on Cameron, thank your father." Mom urged.

"Thanks." He said stifly. What was his problem?"

Dad looked slightly disappointed at Cameron's reaction, and I honestly felt bad since he put in a great amount of effort to give him this car. "...your welcome...why don't you take a little drive around town."

He handed Cameron the keys and Cameron's expression looked like he was disgusted. Ben, Mckenna, and I got in the BMW.

Mckenna and I sat in the back, while Ben sat in the passenger seat. I admired the nice leather seat, and the new car smell.

As we backed out of the driveway I asked Cameron, "What is wrong with you?!" I yelled. "You practically just crushed dad's heart!"

"He can't just buy me fancy stuff and think everything will be okay."

"Cameron, he got you a BEE-EMM-DOUBLE YOU." I emphasized each letter.

"He's just trying to buy my love, which isn't going to work." Cameron said stubbornly, and I rolled my eyes.

"Why do you have to be so difficult?" I mumbled to myself.

"I'm not being difficult, Lizzy, I'm being careful." Cameron answered.

"Careful of what? Making sure dad doesn't buy you common sense next time?" Or even better, a heart to forgive. Ben chuckled quietly, and Mckenna giggled. Cameron glared at me through the rearview mirror in the front.

"He might do something stupid again." Cameron said. I didn't respond back to him. "Then what happens? Mom wants drastic change again, and then we leave everything behind?"

I sighed. In a way Cameron was right. That was the reason why we moved to this albino foundation in the first place, and I hate it here. I'd rather have him than Luke.

As if she read my mind, Mckenna said. "We still have Luke." She said in a cherry voice.

"Ew." I said without thinking.

--

The next morning, I was waiting for Taylor in front of her house so we could walk to school. I was standing out there for about three minutes when Taylor's stepmom came outside with an angry look on her face.

"Can I help you with something?" She asked rudely.

"I was waiting for Taylor..." I said slowly.

"I thought she already told you that I would not allow the two of you to be friends. That includes not walking to school together." She said.

I stared at her for a moment. "I don't seem to understand why." I crossed my arms over my chest.

"People like you aren't worth a dime, even more so, my time." Taylor's step mother said with venom in each word. She stared coldly at me then stormed back into the house, and slammed the door. I felt a lump rise in my throat.

I'm usually a hard person to break, but I had to admit. Those words hurt me a lot. She pretty much called me and any other black person, worthless.

"Fucking bitch." I heard somebody say. I turned around and Cameron was standing next to his BMW with his key in hand, the car door open. "I heard everything." He said.

I sighed and shook my head.

"I'm walking to school with you." Cameron shut the door and put his keys in his pocket.

"You seriously don't have to." I said.

"Well, I want to." He came toward me and put his arm around my shoulder. "Come on little sis."

I smiled. Cameron and I haven't really bonded since we moved here, and he was being extremely nice right now.

"What's the catch?" I asked.

He laughed. "No catch. Watching my sister get treated like shit is the worse thing ever. I'm your big brother, and I'm always there for you."

"Aww, thank you." I said.

"I think mom should talk to Taylor's step mom." Cameron suggested.

I kicked a rock with my foot. "No, that would just make things more worse." I turned to him. "Don't mention it to mom at all, okay?"

"Wouldn't things work out better if she knew?"

"No."

"If you say so.." Cameron said unsure and dropped his arm from my shoulder to adjust his backpack. "You know if things are bothering you, it's best to tell somebody."

I rolled my eyes. "Thanks a lot Dr. Phil."

--

When we got to school, I went to my locker and there was a piece of notebook paper taped to it. YOU DON'T BELONG HEAR [N WORD].

I was slightly amused that whoever took the time to write this couldn't even spell the word 'here' correctly. They even spelled the N word with ONE 'G', so it said Niger like the country.

"Good to know." I said out loud while ripping it off my locker and letting it sway to the floor. I spun my combination and opened my locker.

"What is this?" Turned to see Ben reach down next to me and pick up the paper.

I shrugged and reached up for my books. "It doesn't make sense. It's just..." I couldn't even think of words to describe what I was feeling.

Ben touched my arm. It felt wierd so I flinched. He stared at me for a long time before saying, "Are you okay?"

"Yeah, I actually thought it was funny." I let out a small laugh, but Ben just looked at me with a blank expression. "Or not.." I said awkwardly.

"It's offensive, and I think you should report it." He said with a serious face.

"I would just be wasting my time if I tried to do something about it." I grabbed it from him and crushed it into a paper ball. "Just forget about it." I said while tossing it into my locker.

"Lizzy!" I heard someone yell my name in the hallway. I looked to see Taylor running frantically towards me. Taylor rushed and gave me a hug, nearly knocking me over. "Cameron told me what happened! Im so so so sorry about what my step mom said to you."

"It's not your fault." She still didn't let go of me. "Taylor, relax, it's alright." I noticed Ben was still standing there confused.

She finally let go and looked me straight in the face. "No, it is not alright. Those words were so negative, Lizzy. I feel terrible."

"Do either one of you want to tell me what happened?" Ben asked.

"My racist step mom..." Taylor began to tell Ben what she said. I put my books into my back pack an as Taylor was explaining to Ben I glanced up and noticed Ben's expression. He looked like he felt bad for me. Well I dont need anybody to pity me. I can handle it on my own.

--

During first period, calculus, my teacher was writing a problem on the board. As I was copying, I noticed an error. I raised my hand. The teacher clearly saw my hand raised, but ignored me.

I kept my arm up. "Miss..."

She cut me off. "What do you want Lizzy?" She snapped. Her face was covered with a frown, and the whole class looked at me.

"You made a mistake.." I explained where she messed up and she corrected it on the board.

"Is that better?" She said in a sarcastic tone, but I didn't answer her.

"Oh my freaking goodness." I mumbled and rolled my eyes.

"Huh? I couldn't hear you? Do you want to come up here and teach the class?" Her voice was so ugly. I could not believe how immature my teacher was being right now.

I sighed dramatically. This was honestly unnecesary. "You can continue the lesson, I was just--"

"Do not tell me how to run my lesson." She spat, and walked to her desk and grabbed a piece of paper. She briskly came to my desk and put a detention slip on it. "You will be serving this detention after school today for insubordination."

"Okay." I said.

"No talking back."

"Alright."

"I'll be calling home today."

"Okey dokey." I said just to piss her off and the entire class laughed. She glared at me before turning around and going back up to the board.

Today was just not my day.

--

During lunch I didn't think my day could get any worse, but I was wrong. Erin Maguire approached our table with her little posse following close behind.

"Hey Lizzy." Erin put on a fake smile with her hands rested on her hips.

I just rolled my eyes.

"Did you get our important note?" She asked with a smirk on her face, and I laughed silently in my head. So she was the idiot who couldn't spell, I should have known.

I looked at her and pretended to be confused. "What note? What are you even talking about?" I was definitely not going to give her the benefit of the doubt.

"The one in--" Taylor began, but I cut her off by kicking her chair. She instantly shut her mouth.

"We left it in your locker this morning." A girl with long blonde hair, and a horrible fake tan said.

"Really? My locker? I went to it three times today and didn't find anything." The smirk disappeared from Erin's face and she looked taken a back. "Must have been the wrong locker." I shrugged. "Too bad." I said with authentic sadness in my voice.

Erin scoffed in defeat, flipped her hair over her shoulder, and stormed off. Taylor and the other girl at our table, Alex, burst out laughing.

"I love you Lizzy!" Taylor exclaimed. "You deserve 'best actress' award." After she was finished laughing she said, "I wish I could come over after school."

"I have a detention anyway." I said.

Her eyes went wide. "What? Why?"

"I pointed out a mistake in the calculus notes."

"So?"

"Exactly."

Taylor shook her head. "That is ridiculous." Her gaze went behind me and she sighed.

I followed her gaze behind me to Cameron. He was sitting with Ben and his friends. Erin was standing beside him, her hand was touching Cameron's arm and was desperately flirting with him. "Really Taylor?" I said before turning back around.

"He's so beautiful." She said with this funny smile on her face and I couldn't help but laugh.

Alex laughed and said worriedly, "Erin is pointing at us."

I turned around and Erin, her group, Cameron, and Ben were all staring straight us. I put on a big smile and waved at them across the cafeteria. Erin still had her hands on her hips, with an annoyed expression on her face. Ben and Cameron smiled at waved back.

Making her mad, made me happy.

--

I walked ever so slowly to my detention, taking as little steps as possible. When I got there, only two other people sat in the classroom. A guy....and the teacher. I sighed and signed my name on the detention list. I walked to the back on the class room and took a seat.

"Well this is the biggest detention group I've ever seen." The teacher chuckled and leaned back at his desk with his hands relaxed behind his head.

"Go to hell." I mumbled and the other kid heard and laughed. He was sitting in front of me, and then turned around to face me.

"Hey, cutie what's your name?" He asked in a hispanic accent with a devious grin on his face.

I looked behind me, unsure if he was really talking to me. Then I remembered, I am the only girl in here, let alone student. I stared at him blankly.

"Yeah, I'm talking to you." He let out a soft laugh. "I'm Luis."

"I'm Lizzy." I said with no emotion.

"Well, Lizzy, what brings you to detention this afternoon?" He asked.

"A stupid reason."

"Oh, you got in trouble for breathing too?" He asked sarcastically and I laughed. "Finally, I got a smile." He said.

We sat in silence for a few seconds before he said, "You have beautiful eyes, dark and sexy."

If he wants to flirt with me, he's trying way too hard to do it. "Thanks. I'm flattered." I say sarcastically in response.

He laughed. "You seem like a really cool girl, lizzy. I like cool girls."'

"What are you implying?"

Luis shrugs with his palms out in front of him. "Nothing, I'm just a very observant kind of person."

I laughed. "As I can tell."

"No talking. This is detention." The teacher stated the obvious. Luis winked at me before turning back around in his seat. For the remainder of the detention I put my head down on the desk, and fell asleep.

I felt somebody tap my arm. "Hey, hey Lizzy, we can leave now." I opened my eyes and Luis was hovered over me.

I reached down for my backpack and slung it across my shoulder. I followed Luis out of the class room and pulled out my cellphone. I heard rain fall on the roof, and I was definitely not gonna go through what I did last time it rained. I called Cameron and waited for him to answer.

"Come on Cameron, pick up." I said quietly, but he still didn't answer his phone.

"I can take you home." Luis offered.

"Are you sure?" I asked.

"Sure, it's not a problem mamacita." He said.

I forced a smile, "Thank you." We got outside and it was pouring. Luis and I ran to his car and quickly got inside.

I showed him the easy directions to my house. When he pulled into the driveway the rain subsided, and I noticed Luke's car parked there.

I tried my best to hold in a string of curse words that I was harboring inside. I opened the door. "Thanks for giving me a ride." I say to Luis.

"Anytime." Luis said. As I step out of the car, he grabs my arm. "Hey, we should hangout sometime."

I paused. "Um.." I looked up and noticed Cameron standing on the porch. "I'll see you later, okay?" I quickly got out of Luis's car before he could say anything, and walked to the door.

"Who was that?" Cameron asked.

"A kid named Luis."

Cameron frowned. "What? Are you alright?"

I rolled my eyes, and walked past him to go inside. "What are you even talking about? I told you I had detention. He gave me a ride home."

"Lizzy, I know Luis, and I know about his extremely perverted ways." Cameron said without hesitation.

I laughed. "Don't worry. I don't plan on talking to him anytime soon. Maybe you should have answered your phone when I called you." I took off my coat and hung it on the hook near the door.

"I saw the missed call and figured you needed a ride since it was pouring a few minutes ago. I was on my way to get you.." He explained ,but I stopped listening when I heard Luke's voice come from the kitchen.

I groaned. "Why is he here?" I whispered and Cameron just shrugged. "Ughhhhh!!" I said loudly.

Mckenna came running down the hallway from the kitchen. "Lizzy! You're in trouble!" She said excitedly. WHAT NOW?!

I walked down the hallway with Mckenna and Cameron behind me. Mom and Luke were sitting at the table talking and Mom looked up at me.

"Oh, Lizzy your home. I got a call from your Calculus teacher." Mom had a confused look on her face. "She said you received a detention for back talking, but I didn't quite understand her point."

My jaw dropped. She gave me the detention slip before I even talked back to her. What a liar! "You see ,mom, I kindly informed her that she made a mistake on the board. She gave me the detention form and..."I paused. "I may have slightly talked back to her, but I was responding to what she said."

My mom smiled. "It's alright sweetie. It makes no sense for you to serve a detention for simply making a correction. Do you want me to go talk with the principal or anything?"

"Nope, it's fine." I knew mom wouldn't be upset, and I was feeling a little better about my awful day until words came out of Luke's mouth.

"You shouldn't be disrupting class for such a minor mistake, Lizzy." Luke said. I was about to say something really mean, but I refrained myself.

I turned to Cameron, and gave him a look that signified my annoyance with Luke for getting involved. Every time I see him, I seem to dislike him more and more.

"Oh, come on Luke." My mom intervened. "It's not a big deal."

"Thank you, MOM. People just don't understand." I said shaking my head and looking at Luke to let him know I was personally referring to him.

Cameron pulled my arm. "Come on, before you say something you'll regret , and we definitely don't want that." He said the last quietly.

"Oh, you know me too well." I said.

Chapter 11

jaden pictured above-

"Are you nervous?"

"Nope."

"Really?"

"Nope."

Two weeks later I was sitting on a train with Ben. We were on our way to see Jaden. I didn't want to go alone, and I have been sensing hostility between Cameron and the 'brother' topic. Ben offered to go with me and I accepted. I was extremely nervous and excited at the same time, and I rarely get excited for anything.

"It'll be fine. I promise." Ben tried to reassure me.'

"What if he didn't even know he has a sister?"

"Lizzy, just relax." Ben touch my hand and I flinched. "Why do you always do that?"

"Do what?" I asked nervously.

"When I touch you, you always jump like that. Why?" He asked sounding slightly hurt. His touch is so soft and gentle. It always feels like a shock of electricity is released through out my entire body when I feel his touch. I have no idea why though.

"Uh....uh..I just...it has nothing to do with you. I have quick reflexes." I lied. He didn't say anything so I felt bad. "No really I do. " I sighed and took out my cellphone, i had a text messege from Luis. "Leave me alone."I said out loud. He was honestly starting to annoy me.

"Who?" Ben asked.

"Luis. I met him in detention the other day. He gave me a ride home, and now he thinks i 'want him'. " I made air quotes with my index and middle fingers.

Ben laughed. "Guys like him are not worth your time."

"He's quite the annoyance. He texts me. I don't text back. He keeps texting me." Ben laughed, and I hit him playfully. "It's not funny." I looked up and saw the woman sitting across from me smiling at us.

"You two are such a beautiful couple." She said. Ben and I looked at eachother awkwardly.

"We're not a couple." We both said at the exact same time.

She laughed. "Well you sure fooled me." What was that suppose to mean? I was definitely feeling a little uncomfortable after she said that.

"That just made things awkward.." Ben said.

"Agreed."

--

After we got off the train we took a bus to Jaden's neighborhood. The neighborhood was located in the downtown area, which I was not very familiar with. The bus was full so Ben and I had to stand. I nearly fell several times when the bus turned a corner.

Each time Ben caught me and laughed at me. I rolled my eyes. Holding on to the hand thing was not even helping. I was very grateful once the bus reached our stop.

"I really stand out here." Ben said while glancing awkwardly around. Okay so the neighborhood was a predominantly black area.

"You'll be fine." I looked down at the directions I wrote down on a piece of paper. Jaden's house was just a couple blocks away from the bus stop. The house had three floors and a long staircase leading up to the front door.

"Well this is it." Ben said smiling at me. I just stared blankly at the house. "Lizzy, what are you looking at?"

I shook my head. "I don't want to do this anymore. Let's just go back home." I turned around and began walking.

Ben stopped me before I got any farther. "We can't go back now Lizzy." He said. "You already came this far, Jaden is literally right there." He looked past me at the house.

"I won't know what to say! Should I hug him first when I see him or shake his hand or just not have any physical contact at all?" I spoke quickly, blending all my words together. I couldn't control the nerves. I was so frustrated now. "I didn't know it was going to be this hard, Ben."

Ben laughed put his hands on my shoulders. "Breathe, will you? You sound like my mom when she's bugging me about stupid stuff. The minute you see him, things will all fall into place. "

He had a lot more sense than I thought, and I believed him.

"Now go, before those guys decide to jump me." Ben looked at the four guys sitting on their porch smoking staring intently at us.

This made me laugh so hard. "Okay." I took a deep breath and went back to the house and walked up the stairs. Ben followed close behind me. My heart was beating extremely fast when my finger touched the doorbell.

I heard footsteps come to the door and the door opened, revealing A woman who resembled my biological mother so much.

She smiled. "Lizzy! Welcome!" She motioned excitedly for Ben and I to come in. "I'm Ella."

I could not stop looking at the woman. Her voice still gave chills, and seeing her face made me realize something. "Hi" I said awkwardly. Something was not right.

Ben shook her hand. "Hello, nice to meet you. I'm Ben."

She smiled. "Nice to meet you, Ben." She turned to me and looked at me with a regretful look on her face. "You have grown into a beautiful young woman. You two feel right at home." What was that look for? I was beginning to feel wierd.

"Jaden!" She yelled up the stairs.

"I'm coming!" A boy's muffeled voice came from upstairs. Then he appeared at the top of the stairs. I couldn't help but smile. He looked like me a little. He was taller than I thought he would be.

When he got to the bottom of the stairs I looked at him and he looked back at me. I wanted to hug him. Before I could even move, he came towards me and hugged me. It was probably the most meaningful hug I have ever experienced.

"Aw." I heard his mother sniffle. "You both are going to make me cry."

I surge of relief flooded me. After our hug we stood there staring at ea-chother. He was probably a 3/4 inch shorter than me. He was seemingly taller than the average 13 year old. He had one dimple that formed on the side of his cheek just like I did when I smiled.

"You guys need to be left alone." Ben said. He turned toward Ella. "Would you like any assistance with lunch?"

"You are such a polite young man. Thank you that would be splendid!" Ella beamed and Ben followed her to the back. Leaving me with Jaden.

He laughed nervously. "You look like me."

I smiled. "Technically, YOU look like ME. I was born first."

This struck Jaden as hilarious and he burst out laughing. "You're funny.. ..just like ME." He headed towards the front door. "Do you want to go sit outside."

"Sure." I was pleased that he was not behaving awkwardly around me. One of us had to keep calm, and it definitely was not going to be me. We went outside and walked around to the back of the house to sit on the porch. The neighborhood was quiet except for a few noises in the distance.

Jaden and I sat uncomfortably in silence for moment before he said, "I knew about you for a long time." He picked up a rock and started playing with it. "I've always wanted to know what you were like. I also wanted to know what happened to our...um...mom and dad."

I sighed. "Your mom didn't tell you?"

"She never wanted to talk about them...or you." He looked up at me. "I think she knows something else, but doesn't want to tell me."

Ella. There was something about the way she said things that caught my attention. She may know a lot more about me than I think. Plus, she resembles and sounds like my biological mother so much.

"Well." I began. "It was my birthday, and we went out. On the way home a truck rear-ended our car. It flipped over and...landed in a ditch." Jaden's eyes grew wide. "In the car..." I felt a lump rise in my throat. "I-It was the last time I ever saw you."

"But why?" Jaden's voice shook.

"A social worker said I couldn't see you anymore because our parents were killed, so they had to find somebody to take care of you." I closed my eyes. "And I said 'I need to be with my brother. Please don't take him away.' She told me a nice woman has already came to take care of you. A tear slid down my face and I quickly wiped it away. I hate crying.

"Then I said." I continued. "I asked her 'what about me? Who will take care of me?' But she didn't answer."

"What happened to you after that? Did they find a family for you?" Jaden asked, his face filled with sadness.

"Not right away. I was put in different foster homes for a while before I was finally adopted."

"And I thought I had it rough." He mumbled.

I let my gaze fall to his legs. "You broke both of your legs, Jaden." I laughed. "That's pretty rough."

His eyes got wide. "Yeah and now they look crooked!" He stretched his legs out straight and pulled up the pant legs of his jeans. "See!" I noticed that they were not as straight as they should be but they were barely noticeable.

"Nobody will know unless they stare for a very long time." I said. "And if they do just tell them to kiss your a....I mean butt." I quickly corrected myself.

Jaden burst into a fit of laughter then said, "Did you break anything from the accident?"

"Four of my ribs were crushed..."

"What?!" Jaden exclaimed. "Your ribs!"

I laughed. "It sounds really bad, huh. I had to wear a brace thing for my chest. It hurt to breath, cough, and laugh." I placed my left hand over my right rib cage. "It's all healed now, but sometimes if I laugh too hard or somebody hits me too hard it aches a little." I smiled. "But I'm fine now. I still laugh extremely hard and ignore slight pain."

"I didn't hurt you when I hugged you, did I?"

"Of course not." I said as I outstretched my arms and hugged him.

"Aww isn't that just a beautiful moment." I heard someone murmur. I turned towards the house to see Ella poking her head out of a window. "Come inside cuties!" Ella yelled out the kitchen window at us.

"Coming." I said as Jaden and I stood up.

"What's your boyfriends name?" Jaden asked.

I was confused. "What boyfriend?"

"The one you came with."

"Oh, you mean Ben. He's not my boyfriend, I guess..he's a friend of mine."
I said.

Jaden smiled coyly. "Sure. What ever you say Lizzy."

I laughed and gave him a playful shove. "I'm being honest." We reached the
kitchen and Ella and Ben were engaged in a conversation, but they stopped
once we walked in.

"How did it go?" Ben whispered to me.

"Lets just say you were right." I admitted and he laughed. "What did you
and Ella talk about?"

"Don't worry about it." Ben said and I rolled my eyes in annoyance. He is
always doing this to me.

"I want to talk to Lizzy." Ella smiled at me.

"But we weren't even done talking, mom." Jaden whined.

"Don't worry. I will let you two finish up later. Jaden take Ben down to the
basement, you guys can play call of duty."

"You have call of duty?" Ben turned to Jaden. "I love you man." I rolled my
eyes as they both hurried down to the basement.

Ella motioned for me to sit down at the table, and I did while she got me a
glass of water. "Did you have any trouble getting down here?"

I laughed nervously. "So I'm not used to public buses." I took a sip of water.

Ella laughed. "You don't take it often?"

"No, not really since I live in the suburbs."

Ella's smile quickly faded. "So you mean, you live in a white area?"

"Mostly."

Ella closed her eyes for a second before opening them again. "Sweetie, Please don't tell me your family is white."

I swallowed hard and eyed her suspiciously. "Yes." I said unsure if I should have told her the truth.

"Well I'll be damned." She said. "Those folks better be treating you right! I knew I should have adopted you too. Lynette would never forgive me for letting you go!"

My breath caught in my throat. "Excuse me?" Lynette was my biological mother's name. "You knew our mother?"

Ella covered her mouth after she realized what she had said. "Oh dear." She shook her head. "I didn't want to tell you like this but...your mother.." she trailed off.

"Yes?"

" she and I were sisters"

Chapter 12

"WHAT!?" I did intend for that to come out as a yell, but I was shocked. I really didn't know what else to do or say at that moment. I had thought all this time I had no living relatives, but now I find out that Ella is my aunt. This would explain why she looks and sounds like my biological mom.

"Now listen to me Lizzy, I.." Ella began

I then stopped listening to her. My head began to pound and I groaned. "Do you have anything I can take for this headache?"

She abruptly shut her mouth, surprised by my irrelevent question. "Oh hunny, I'll be right back." As she walked past she rubbed my shoulder while I sat with my forehead resting in my palm.

She returned with a bottle of asprin and set it down on the table in front of me. She rubbed my back before returning to her seat across the table. I shook two pills into my palm from the bottle and put them in my mouth. I took my glass of water and swallowed.

Ella watched me and nodded her head violently. "You and Jaden both have those horrible headaches. You get it from your mom."

"Why didn't anybody tell me about you?" I blurted out.

Ella sighed. "Nobody knew. Your mom and I weren't exactly close, but I'd do anything for her." I ran my fingers against the glass filled with water. "The accident was in the newspaper the following morning. I still have it somewhere in this place." She glanced around. "I saw your mother and father's name and I knew they had two children." She paused. "I didn't hesitate to call the hospital and ask about you guys. I talked to several social workers and the adoption angency. I was gonna take you both." Ella stopped again and sniffled.

I waited for her to continue and she finally did. "I was gonna adopt you and Jaden but the adoption agency was being so picky! They said I didn't make enough money to provide for two kids so I could only take one of you." Tears began falling down Ella's face.

I looked around and saw a box of tissues down the hallway in the living room. The chair creaked as I quickly got up to get the box and bring it to her. She dabbed at her eyes, but continued to sob.

"Thank you sweetie." She said between sobs. "I fought and fought to have you both, but they just would not let me. I had to choose. The reason why I took Jaden was because he was so young. The agency said it would be easier since he most likely won't remember anything. But in the hospital all Jaden kept saying was 'Izzy, Izzy' and it killed me to leave you behind."

Ella sighed. "Ever since then not a day went by that I did not think about you. Where you were, if you were being fed. Even when I got that phone call about you, I was thinking about how much you must have grown earlier that day." She smiled regretfully. "When I opened the door and saw you I felt so guilty. You are such a beautfiful young lady . I could have raised you and been there for you."

I let out a shaky breath and licked my lips. "Why didn't you contact me sooner?"

"I didn't know what to tell you if I did. He eventually forgot about you and his parents. I waited about 8 years before I finally told Jaden about everything and he was so angry with me. I kept the fact that I'm his aunt away from him."

My eyes went wide. "So he doesn't know?" Ella shook her head sadly. "Wow." That was all I managed to say.

"Did they put you in a foster home?" She asked.

I nodded. "Yeah, two terrible ones."

"Lizzy, I am truly sorry. I am so sorry for letting all this happen to you. Can you ever forgive me?" Fresh tears were falling down Ella's face. Her face that reminded me so much of my mom.

"Ella." I said and she stopped sobbing and looked at me. "C-Can I please... hug you?" She stood up and outstretched her arms to me. I tightly wrapped my arms around her and memories of my mom flooded back to me. Ella was about the same size as she was and her voice was identical.

"Oh Elizabeth. I'm sorry I left you. I am always here if you need me, ok?" Ella spoke softly and I closed my eyes and listened to her voice, imagining it was mom speaking to me. "I love you and Jaden so much. I never wanted you to feel alone. Please don't be mad."

"It's not your fault." I let go of her and stepped back to look at her. "I could never be mad at you. I want to thank you for taking care of my brother, Auntie Ella."

Ella smiled and quickly sat down. She dragged me over to her so I could sit on her lap. I started laughing because I felt like a little kid all over again. "Now tell me Lizzy, does Ben go to school with you?"

I let out a nervous laugh. "Yeah he lives across the street from me, why?"

"Girl, he is so handsome. I thought he was your boyfriend when you guys walked in!" Her voice was ecstatic.

I sighed and rolled my eyes. "Oh gosh." Why is today the only day that I'm hearing this about Ben and I. This is the THIRD TIME TODAY!

"But he told me you guys weren't dating." Ella reassured me.

I gasped. "You asked him?!" She nodded shyly and we both burst out laughing. After a few minutes of talking I went down to the basement to see what the boys were up to. They were sitting on the couch, laughing hysterically and fully engrossed in their game until Jaden spotted me.

"I'll be right back Ben." He said quickly, and paused the game. "Don't start it until i get back." He rushed past me up the stairs. He probably wanted to give me and my supposed boyfriend time alone.

Ben chuckled shouted,"Don't worry, I won't." He rested his arms behind his head, leaned back on the couch and looked at me. "Hey." He said.

"Hi." I went and plopped down on the floor in front of his feet. "Are you guys playing black tops?"

Ben blinked twice and stared at me like he couldn't believe what I just said. "You mean black ops..."

I shrugged and leaned back on my hands. I didn't know about this crap. "Yeah, yeah you know what I meant" I mumbled. "Hows it coming along?"

"Good, good. How did it go with Ella?"

I made an obnoxious sound with my lips. "Let's just say my mind was blown. I'll save you the details for later, because it's ..too much. She even had to get me aspirin."

"Seriously?" Ben leaned forward with his elbows resting on his knees. "Are you okay? Is everything alright? We heard you yell and we heard Ella crying. Is she okay?"

I nodded. "I'll let you know everything, I promise." There was a silence between us and Ben's gaze went to the floor. I took this opportunity to look at Ben. I mean really look at him. I noticed how muscular he actually was. His arms were slightly buff, causing the sleeves of his black shirt to hug his arms. And there was no doubt he had a nice set of abs, I could tell even with his shirt on. He had a nicely structured jawline, also. He had a good looking face too, and those brown eyes. Those same brown eyes that he looked at me with.

It took me a moment to finally realize that Ben is SEXY AS HELL! This never occurred to me because I never took the time to look. I stared at his facial features once again and this time Ben's gaze met my eyes, he caught me staring!

I panicked and forced a smile. He smiled back at me and chuckled. "You okay?" He asked and I simply nodded. He was very attractive and he had a cute smile. Oh and that deep voice is so sexy.

UGH WHAT AM I DOING. I felt somewhat guilty for studying him like this, but since I kept hearing all these things about Ben and I, I had to actually think about what they were saying.

Hm, his name should be Ben 10 like the cartoon. Because SHAWTY IS DEFINITELY A 10 PLUS!

What kind of aspirin did I take?

--

The following Monday at school, Luis approached me suddenly. "Hey Lizzy."

I took a step back and said nervously, "Hey Luis."

"Have you been getting my text messages?" He asked.

"Yeah, I have."

Luis stared at me for a moment. Then he chuckled softly. "Are you avoiding me?"

"I-I've just had a lot going on, that's all. You know things get pretty busy, but I'm really sorry, Luis." I paused trying to think of something to say. "There's not much to say when we talk, because we barely know eachother."

Luis took a step closer to me and a devious smirk covered his face. "Well, mamacita, we can get to know eachother." Then he leaned his face close to mine and whispered, "With our clothes on or off. It's only between us."

It took all I had not to laugh in his face. I shifted my weight from my left leg to my right and just sighed, "Luis.."

He cut me off by putting his index finger to my lips, "Shh." I violently smacked his hand away. "It's okay if you want me, Lizzy." He continued.

"First of all, don't tell me to SHH! Second of all, I DO NOT WANT YOU. And third of all, I'm going to be late to class if I keep talking to you, so Adios amigo!" I waved my hand in his face as I started walking away.

"ooh, I like a fiesty girl." I heard him say. "And a girl who can speak my language."

I just rolled my eyes and continued to walk down through the crowded hall way. Down the hall I noticed Ben, Ryan, Kevin, and Cameron talking. I abruptly stopped and went the other direction. I do not know why, but ever since I noticed how VERY attractive Ben was, i've been feeling guilty for some reason. I feel like I can't have a civilized conversation with him without thinking about how good he looks.

Taylor must be rubbing off on me.

--

Saturday morning I woke up, took a shower and got dressed. I brushed my hair and put on a yellow headband to match my yellow shirt. When I walked out of my room I saw Ben jogging up the stairs and I froze. I hadn't really talked to him since I realized how hot he is. It just feels wierd now for some reason. It's not that I'm falling in love with him or anything, it's his good looks that are driving me insane. Am I beginning to like him? How could I have missed this before. And seeing him jogging up the stairs looked like something out of a movie. The only thing missing was the slow motion effect and dramatic music.

"Hey stranger. Where have you been?" He asked. "It feels like we haven't talked in days." That's probably because we hadn't talked in days.

I leaned my back against the wall. "Hey. Uh..I've been alright. Um...how have y-you been?"

He eyes me suspiciously. "What's with you?"

"Um n-nothing."

"You're acting different." He came up to me and rested his arms above my head on the wall, trapping me in between. Ben was a couple inches taller than me. He stared down at me, his face centimeters away from mine. "Do I make you nervous or something?" He asked quietly. Nervous? Is that how

I sounded? Why would I be nervous around Ben? I've never been this close to him before.

I tried to steady my breathing. His scent filled my nose; he smelled so good. I could tell he was wearing Axe cologne. From the corner of my eyes I could see his muscular arms. Then I snapped back into reality and finally said, "What? No!" I managed to squeeze my way from in between him and the wall, and moved around him.

Ben removed his hands from the wall and turned to face me. "You're never like this." He said.

I scrunched my eyebrows together. "Like what?"

"Like this." Ben motioned his hand toward me. he stared straight into my eyes as if trying to see my soul. i tried to challenge him by staring back but i got this funny feeling and quickly looked away and crossed my arms over my chest.

"Maybe a little partying will put you in the right mood." Ben said with a devious grin on his face.

"Party? What party?" I asked confused.

"Ryan is having a party at his house tonight. His parents are out of town.." He paused, "yeah you know what teens usually do. Cameron and I were planning on going." He continue to look at me as if I was insane. "And judging by the way you're behaving, you should come too."

I pondered on his offer and thought 'what harm could be done?'

"Sure." I said.

--

I was definitely not going to go through this party without Taylor, so I got her to come along. Taylor, Ben, Cameron, and I had arrived thirty minutes ago. From the moment I entered, I was entirely horrified. There were guys and girls making out everywhere. Body shots on the kitchen counter, and dozens of intoxicated teens. It seemed like the entire school was here.

Ben and Cameron ventured off somewhere, which left Taylor and I roaming through the crowds. We ended up in the back yard where fewer people were. We sat on a swinging bench and just watched everyone.

This partially sober guy approached us with two drinks in his hand. "You ladies want a drink?" He asked.

"Sure!" Taylor said excitedly and took the plastic, red cup from him. He then walked away looking dazed.

I smacked the side of her arm. "Taylor! You're not suppose to take drinks from people!"

"Lizzy, we need to have some fun. Don't be such a party pooper!" She took a swig from the cup. "Ahh." She sighed.

"There's more where that came from!" The drunk guy called from across the lawn.

"ooh. Be right back Lizzy." She said after drinking the rest of the liquid inside the cup. I stared at her in disbelief as she went to get more.

If Taylor seemed like the one not to party. You are terribly mistaken. This girl started dancing with some guy who was in my english class. She began to grind all up on him! She was giggling,

I had enough. I got up off the bench and went near her. I grabbed this random guy's hand to dance, but not really. I began to move a little to the rhythm. I just wanted to tell Taylor something, but do that in a non obvious way.

"I like girls who make the first move. Dang you can dance too." The guy said. "I'm Jake by the way." He said moving along with me.

I just rolled my eyes and ignored him. "Taylor!" I hissed through the blaring music.

"I'm having so much fun wooo!" Taylor began fist pumping out of no where. This girl is so wild!

"Can you please control yourself!" I said then Taylor abruptly stopped dancing and had a funny expression on her face. She darted away towards the inside of the house but didn't make it time.

She grabbed a potted plant off the ground and began to vomit in it. I went over to her. "Come on, let's get out of here." I pleaded with her.

"Lizzzzzy, sssstop it." Taylor slurred. "Leave my intoxicated ssself alone!"

"Wow. I'll be in the bathroom. If I'm not back in five minutes, call the police." I said sarcastically. Sarcasm probably isn't the best way to communicate with a drunk person because all taylor did was throw up more inside the potted plant. Poor little plant.

I found a bathroom down the hallway. I knocked, but I heard moaning sounds coming from inside. I quickly turned away and went upstairs to find another bathroom. I found one upstairs at the end of the hall and after I was done in there I walked out.

I then felt arms come around my waist and a hand covered my mouth. I was being pulled away and I couldn't even react.

chapter 13

I began to kick around as hard as I could and tried to pry whoever's hand that was off my face. I was pulled into a bedroom nearby. The room was the size of a master bedroom. It had a large bed in the center with a single lamp on in the darkened room.

"You're a tough one, chica." As soon as he said that, I knew it was Luis. I could smell a hint of alcohol from his breath. This made me even more furious. I managed to kick him right in the groin and he cursed in pain. His grip around me loosened and I took that opportunity to sprint to the door of the bedroom.

I had to take a moment to unlock the door, but as soon as I was about to open it Luis came up behind me and slammed it shut. He then stood in front the door, locking it again and blocking me from trying to leave.

"What is wrong with you! Are you insane?! Let me out right now, Luis. I'm not even kidding." I said sternly.

"Don't you want to have some fun with me?" He asked. "Let'ssss play a game."

I rolled my eyes."Just think of me as the Barbie you will never get to play with. Move out of my way, now." I said as I tried to move past him to the door. Luis still wouldn't let me by. He had a smirk on his face. I gave him a cold stare and then let out a long, loud bloodcurling scream. Even Luis jumped a bit.

He looked startled and then clamped his hand over my mouth. Hopefully somebody heard me. "You shouldn't do that, chica. We don't want to be interrupted." Without warning he grabbed me and pushed me all the way to the bed.

"HELPPP!" i screamed loudly. Luis suddenly got on top of me and crashed his lips onto mine. GROSS. I tried to aim for his crotch again but he was better prepared this time, and made sure I wasn't able to kick him down there.

I managed to shove him away a little and looked at him. "Why are you doing this?!" I asked. "I can find you a girl if you are really that desperate."

"But what if it's you that I want?" He said looking down at me with menacing eyes.

"But what if it's ME that you can not have!" I retorted loudly in his face. At that moment, We heard a noise at the door.

Luis turned and looked towards the door. "Shh." He said to me and put his finger to my lips. I smacked it way in anger.

The door knob wiggled. "Hey! Why is my parents bedroom locked? Whose in there?" It was Ryan's voice. He began to pound violently on the door. "Get out! This room is off limits!"

Luis clamped his hand over my mouth again to prevent me from scream- ing. He got off of me and pulled me to my feet, still careful to keep my mouth covered. He then took me away from the bed. I looked at the lamp and without thinking I did some amazing ninja move and kicked the lamp to the ground. It made a lot of noise. ALOT.

"I'm going to drop kick whoever's ass is in there!" Ryan yelled from the other side of the door. I could hear him fumbling with the doorknob to get it open.

"Hey, I need to get going. Have you seen Lizzy?" I heard Ben's voice and I felt happy suddenly.

"Not now, Ben. I'm getting these idiots in my parents room out of here." Just then the bedroom door flew open.

Free at last!

"What the hell? Lizzy are you okay?" Ryan said and made his way toward us, but Luis let go of me and dashed towards the door.

Ben stopped him by connecting his fist with luis jaw. I gasped. Luis stumbled back onto the floor clutching his face. Ben stared at Luis coldly then looked up at me. His expression turned into a smile.

"You ready to get out of here?" He asked casually as if he hadn't just punched somebody in the face. I simply nodded.

Just then Taylor and Cameron walked in. "Sssso the party is ssup here nowww?" Cameron slurred. Then through the window we saw red and blue flashing lights.

"Uh oh its the Police!!" Somebody yelled from downstairs.

"CRAP! who called the cops?!" Ryan yelled frantically and ran outside the room.

Taylor looked at me confused. "I thought that's what you wanted me to do Lizzy." PARTY'S OVER.

Life lesson: it is indeed a bad idea to communicate sarcasm with a drunk person.

--

It was 4am, sunday morning. I lay wide awake in my bed listening to the loud rhythmic snoring from Taylor right beside me. She couldn't go home as drunk as she was so she is sleeping over. Ben, also, was sleeping in Cameron's room.

We made it out of Ryan's house without getting caught by the police, but they found the alcohol and called his parents. So, i'm guessing he's in a bunch of trouble.

I don't know why I can't fall asleep though. I just keep thinking about Luis and how psychotic he gets when he's drunk, and how close he was to take advantage of me. And Ben. There's something about him.He's so nice and car....WHACK!

My thoughts were interrupted by Taylor's arm swinging over and smacking me right in the face. I must admit, that did hurt. Taylor, being so oblivious in her sleep just continued to snore. I slowly got out of bed and decided to sleep on the couch in the loft out in the hallway.

When I walked down the hallway I noticed the couch was already preoc-cupied. Ben was laying there with one arm resting behind his head, staring at the wall. He sort of looked upset.

"Ben? What are you doing out here?" I asked confused and switched on the dim light on the hallway.

"Your brother sounds like a dying whale when he snores." He said as he sat up. "You can't sleep either?"

"Yeah, Taylor is a pretty..wild sleeper." He chuckled, but it sounded forced.

"Is something bothering you?" I went and sat next to him on the couch and shifted so I had one leg bent so I was facing him.

Ben looked straight ahead and shook his head, "What happened at the party, It was my fault. If I hadn't told you to come then-" I cut him off.

"What! No! Ben, are you kidding? it was not your fault at all. Luis es loco!" I expected him to laugh at me like he usually did, but he didn't.

Ben finally looked at me. "Did he hurt you? I swear I can do so much more damage."

"He would have." I paused and then glanced at the floor. "But you and Ryan came at the right time, Ben. Thank you for punching Luis in the face." I said gratefully.

I heard him laugh. "It was my pleasure."

"Thank you so much...for everything." My thoughts went back to Jaden and how Ben supported me the whole way. Then, I do not know what foreign force took over me, but somehow my arms found their way around Ben's torso and I was hugging him. Something I've never done with him before.

It took a moment for Ben to even react, but when he did he wrapped his arms around me and rubbed the side of my arm affectionately. It wasn't cold, but his touch gave me chills. This time I didn't flinch or move away. His embrace made me feel amazing.

I felt Ben gently kiss the side of my head. Oh my goodness. I nearly melted. I slowly released my arms from around him before my emotions would leave me forever in his arms.

I looked up at him. "You need to get some rest. I'll just sleep downstairs. You were here first." I stood up, but Ben held my hand.

"Don't be crazy," He said. "This couch is big enough for two people. Come here." Ben gently pulled me back down and scooted over so I could lay down next to him. I just couldn't resist.

"Come on. You can use my broad chest as a pillow." He said and I laughed. All the nervous feelings I had just vanished and they were replaced with comfortable ones. I rested my head on his chest and I could hear the steady beating of his heart.

"Are you comfortable?" He asked.

"Mhm" VERY.

Ben wrapped his arms around me and caressed the side of my arm. "Good-night, Lizzy." He said softly, and before I knew it, I fell into a deep, peaceful sleep.

--

The sound of giggling woke me up that morning. I slowly opened my eyes and my little sister Mckenna was creepily kneeling on the floor beside the couch at my eye level staring back at me.

Then I remembered where I was and who I fell asleep next to earlier that morning and instantly shot up. Ben was no longer there. I looked left and right and down the hallway frantically.

"Where is everybody?" I asked her.

"Mommy's in the kitchen making breakfast for us and Ben and Taylor." She giggled again.

I rolled my eyes. "Why are you giggling so much?" I stood up and stretched my arms above my head.

"Because we saw you." She simply said.

"Who saw what?" I asked confused.

"Me, mommy, Cameron, and Taylor saw you and Ben sleeping here on the couch together." Mckenna bounced around like she usually did. I guess that's her way of dancing.

I stared at her wide eyed. OH NO. Everybody saw! I wonder what they all were thinking. It took me a moment to realize the shower was running. I wonder who was taking a shower. My head is spinning.

I intensely marched to Cameron's door. I put my ear to the door and didn't hear anything so I just opened the door. LOW AND BEHOLD I see Cameron and Taylor making out on his bed. This is Taylor and Cameron. Taylor as in the one who is in love with Cameron and could barely talk to him. I couldn't even speak because I was in shock. They didn't even notice I had walked in. What has this world come to?

"Wow.." Was all I managed to say before I insanely darted out of the room. As I turned around I bumped into something wet. It took me a minute to realize I collided with a person.

Ben.

A shirtless Ben.

A wet bodied Ben.

With a towel wraped around his waist.

And his 8 pack masculine structure exposed.

SWEET JESUS.

Once again, I became mute suddenly. This was all too much to handle in one moment. Taylor and Cameron Kissing, Ben shirtless, and me feeling embarrased and Confused at the same time.

"Sorry." I said in the tiniest voice and ran to my bedroom down the hall. I shut the door and locked it. I didn't come out for a while.

Two hours later a knock came at my door. I was laying helplessly on my bed in misery. I was feeling hungry too!

"Yeah?" I said.

"Open the door Lizzy." I heard Cameron say.

"No." I retorted.

"Hangovers are so terrible." Taylor groaned. "Please, Lizzy. We will explain everything, just let us in." Taylor also sounded miserable.

"But you also have some explaining to do." Cameron sounded angry.

"Explain what?!" I shouted.

Cameron's voice could have broken my door down when he said,"WHY YOU AND BEN WERE SLEEPING TOGETHER!"

Ooops. I forgot about that.

"Where is he?" I asked squeezing my arms around my pillow.

There was a pause, "He's not around so let us come in." Taylor pleaded. I was starving so I willingly got up out of my bed and unlocked the door and before I could full pull it open, Cameron, Taylor AND BEN came busting through my door.

"Hey! You lied!" I shouted. Cameron spun my computer chair around and sat on it backward facing my bed. Taylor sat on my bed. Ben sat on the floor against the wall and I couldn't even look at him now. I felt like I had violated him. I decided to sit as far away as possible from him on my bed.

"Now. Lizzy, I've already interrogated the mess out of Ben, but I need to hear it from you too." Cameron said watching me intently.

"What?" I asked annoyed.

"Why did you two leave your designated sleeping locations and go to the loft?"

I sighed, "Because you and Taylor sound like pigs when you sleep," I glanced at Taylor. "And you hit me so hard in the face I saw stars!" I exclaimed and Cameron and Ben laughed.

Cameron's smile quickly faded and his expression turned serious. "Did anything happen between you two on that couch?"

"We slept. That's all." I managed to look at Ben. "Ri...right?" I stuttered.

"Right." He said. Aw why wasn't he saying much? Oh wow he looks nice right now, Dang I ne-.

"What are you looking at!?" Cameron asked in raged.

"Huh? What? Nothing!" I quickly took my eyes off Ben. "Nothing happened! So leave it alone! How about you tell me why I saw you and Taylor making out? Explain that one!"

"You see," Taylor Began. "I woke up." She used hand gestures to tell this story as if it were really that dramatic. "And you were no where to be found. So I decided to go find Cameron. So I went to his room, knocked on the door. He opened it. One thing lead to another..."

"You can stop right there." I said disgusted and looked at Cameron. "I don't understand why you're making a big out of the fact that we were just sleeping on the couch."

"Because you were nearly raped last night by Luis! And, by the way, remind me to rearrange his face, chop off his balls, and poke out his eyes." Cameron said. I'm guessing Ben informed him about what happened, since he was too drunk to even function last night.

"And guess who saved me? It was not you, was it?" I asked rhetorically, and it left Cameron looking dumb. "Right." I got off my bed. "Now can you all please leave." I avoided looking in Ben's direction. I could feel him staring at me.

"Can I talk to you, Lizzy?" I heard Ben ask. I unwillingly looked at him. Bad Idea since all I could picture was him in that towel. Damn.

"Su..sure." I stuttered again, feeling embarrassed all over again.

Cameron got off my chair and looked at Ben up and Down. "Make it quick." He said.

Taylor got up off my bed too and gave me a look of adoration and mouthed the words, "He really cares about you." and followed Cameron out the door. I wasn't sure who she was even talking about. Cameron in a brotherly form or..Ben?

The room was silent when it was Ben and me alone. I used a pillow and covered my face with it so he wouldn't see me freak out behind it.

"Lizzy?" He asked.

"Yep?" My muffled voice sounded.

"You don't have to feel embarrassed in front of me."

I cleared my throat. "I didn't mean to bump into you. It was an accident."

"I know. It was awkward but, " He stopped. "It's like I'm talking to a pillow." Ben muttered. "Please let me see your beautiful face, Lizzy." Did

Ben just call me, Lizzy West, beautiful? I silently squealed in my head. "Please?" He asked again.

I slowly put the pillow down and looked at him. I was blushing, but he would never know. The benefits of being black..

"Um, like I was saying..." His voice trailed off. "What was I saying?" I just shrugged and shook my head. "Lizzy, you are making this so awkward. Quit being shy and say something."

"I think I like you." I blurted out.

And let the troubles begin.

What did you think? So, I was wondering if you all would like me to include Ben's point of view occasionally? Comment please, I love reading them and seeing what you all think will happen. Ha. Feel free to recommend my story to others. Thanks guys :)

Chapter 14

I know you guys hate me soooo much. I'm so sorry haha

--

My mouth.

My big, stupid mouth.

After I realized those words had actually left my mouth I quickly said, "Oh my goodness, what did I just say?" Ben's expression was covered with shock. He did not even look at me now.

I buried my face in the pillow. "What have I done? What Have I done? What have I done?" I repeatedly mumbled into the pillow. I couldn't even look at Ben now either. With my head down, I felt movement in my room and felt my bed shift. Ben was sitting next to me now, I knew.

I felt his hand gently caress my back and I shivered. I felt him lean in and kiss the side of my head and whisper into my ear,

"I think it's finally safe for me to say...I like you too."

My heart melted beyond its melting point now and I didn't even know what to do or how to react to what Ben had just confessed to me. I slowly lifted my head up and looked at him.

"Are you joking?" I asked.

Ben looked surprised by question, "Does it really look like I'm joking, Lizzy?"

I didn't say anything and looked straight ahead and stared at the wall. I heard Ben sigh next to me. Probably out of confusion and frustration. I then felt his hand gently cup my chin and turn my head to face him and the next thing I remember is him planting the sweetest, most gentle kiss on my lips.

When we finally parted, his face was inches away from mine; he was staring at me straight in the eye and asked "Do you still think I'm joking?"

I giggled nervously and shook my head. I was feeling all giddy after he kissed me. He smiled and pulled me closer to him. Ben wrapped his arms around me.

"Oh lizzy..." Ben said and chuckled.

"What's so funny?" I asked.

"Cameron is going to kill us."

--

It was already Monday morning. This past weekend a lot happened, not only between Ben and I but also Taylor and Cameron. Ben and I told everyone that we were in a relationship now. Everyone took it well, my mom was excited, but Cameron had to take some time to adjust to it. I also had to get used to the fact that Taylor and Cameron were a thing too.

I had no idea he liked her all this time, could you blame me? He spent most of his time kissing Erin.

The only thing I dreaded about today was how things would be at school. People will stare and talk about Ben and I. Ben has a good reputation and dating me might change that. What if he doesn't even wanna claim me?

I shook those thoughts from my head and put my backpack on. Ben would probably meet me at my locker or something so I should start walking now.

"Cameron I'm gone!" I shouted as I ran down the stairs.

"Alright! See ya!" He called back.

I went out the door and I noticed Ben's car still in the driveway. Maybe he's running late today, I shrugged and began walking.

"Liz! Hang on!" I stopped and saw Ben jog quickly out of his house to my side. "Hey how are you?" He asked breathless and gave me a quick peck on the lips.

"I'm fine. What are you doing? Why haven't you left for school yet?"

"I was waiting for you. You thought I was actually gonna drive and let you walk alone?" He took my hand and we began walking "Crazy girl." He chuckled and I laughed.

"Aw ." I said. As we were walking we both became silent.

"Something is bothering you." Ben said confidently.

I looked up at him "What?"

"Tell me."

I sighed, "People are gonna talk when they see you with me, Ben. Doesn't that bother you?"

Ben abruptly stopped walking. "Let them talk Lizzy. It doesn't bother me one bit." He pulled me into a hug. "Don't worry about it, alright?

"Alright."

A car passing by suddenly slowed down next to us and rolled down their tinted windows and looked at us, I didn't recognize the platinum blonde driving the car but she said ,"Ben, what are you doing?"

Ben turned to face her "Hugging my girlfriend. What does it look like?"

"It looks like your sympathizing the black girl. You're lucky it was me who saw you. Don't let anybody see you doing this again." She looked directly at me, "Oh and black girl, stay away from our boys." She rolled up her window and sped off towards the school up ahead.

My mouth hung open in astonishment. "I knew this would never ever work out." I said and let go Of Ben's hand and continued walking briskly to the school.

"Lizzy, please wait, please. I'm so sorry about what she said. I really don't care. Please, this is going to work out. Trust me." He said trying to grab my arm. "Lizzy please....I.." He looked at me like he was literally about to cry.

"Ben, we have only publicized our relationship for 5 minutes and it is already being frowned upon. I don't know if I can take this."

"I know, Lizzy, I know. It'll get better; this is only the first day." He said trying to reassure me, but I truly didn't believe that.

--

As we walked the hallways together people were either talking about the party Saturday night or calling me names and saying terrible things about Ben and I. Ben just shrugged it all off, I would have too, but it was really killing me inside. During the passing period we got stares as we stopped at his locker.

"Did we have homework in Chemistry?" Ben asked as he was pulling things out of his locker. I just shrugged, not really listening to him. Suddenly he stepped aside and pushed me against the locker and we began kissing. I heard gasps come from several people in the hallway.

I stopped for a moment and quietly asked, "What are you doing?"

Ben grinned, "Giving them all something to talk about," then he proceeded to kiss me passionately again. I must admit, I love this rough side of Ben.

He pulled away for a moment and looked at me and smiled. He quickly pecked my lips one last time and moved away. Ben picked up his backpack, slammed his locker shut and took my hand in his.

Ben's actions made me see how proud he was to have me, but how much longer would we have to go through this?

--

I walked into the cafeteria and was instantly attacked by racial slurs and profanity and I went to my lunch table and found Alex and Taylor. "So is it true? You and Ben really are dating?" Alex asked in shock.

"Yes it's true! And I'm so unbelievably happy for them!" Taylor squealed. I forced a smile.

"How are people taking you and Cameron?" I took out my packed sandwich and took a bite.

"Well....Erin and her crew hate me! I have haters, Lizzy! And it feels great! I have something that they want, but can't have." Taylor squealed. "I'm so happy." At least one of us was enjoying their day.

I saw people approach our table at the corner of our eyes. It was Ben, Cameron, Ryan, and Kevin carrying their lunch trays.

"Hey ladies," Kevin said as they all took a seat at our table. Ben pulled a chair and sat next to me, Cameron did the same next to Taylor, and the two others sat on either side of Alex.

"Hey," we said kind of awkwardly in unison.

Ben rubbed my arm and kissed my forehead. He was always providing me with a comforting feeling. Always, and I loved it. I expected lunch to be awkward but it really wasn't. We all were talking excitedly, eating, and laughing like nothing changed. The only difference would be the new addition to our outcast table. Are we still even outcasts?

Probably.

The cafeteria stared over at our table like bees had invaded it, but nobody at the table seemed to mind. Then Erin and her posse came up to the table with their arms folded at their chests.

"Guys, what is going on? Why are you sitting here?!" Erin shrieked. "Is it really true? I thought it was some lame joke."

"Not a joke." Cameron said before taking a bite out of his pizza.

"It's true." Ben said after taking a gulp from his water bottle.

"Very true." Kevin and Ryan said simultaneously.

I just continued to eat my sandwich.

"Wow...Cameron. Okay what about all those times we made out in the hallway?" Erin asked.

Cameron laughed, "Oh yeah, that probably will never happen again. That was a mistake." He looked over at Taylor next to him and gave her a peck on the lips.

"Really? I think the biggest mistake you and Ben have made is dating these two losers. Especially that black one over there." She smirked while she looked at me.

Ben stood up so fast I was shocked. He stood face to face with Erin. "Hey Erin, if you say anything about Lizzy ever again I promise you.." He leaned closer to her and whispered something in her ear which made her mouth open wide.

"You wouldn't!" Erin exclaimed.

Ben smiled and sat down "I would. Now shut that damn mouth of yours closed and go elsewhere."

She gasped and walked fast away from our table with her friends following close behind.

"What did you say to her?" I asked.

"If she ever says anything to you again, you'll find out."

"High five!" I said and he smacked my hand and we laughed.

"How do you girls just take that crap that Erin says?" Kevin asked.

Taylor, Alex and I exchanged glances, "You get used to it after a while, I guess." Alex said.

Ryan turned to look at her, "You're cute, and you don't deserve that." We all stopped what we were doing and looked at Ryan confused about what he had just said.

"What?" Alex asked.

"What? I mean you all are beautiful ladies and don't deserve it." He laughed nervously and stood up, "Anybody want me to throw away their trash for them?" We piled stuff onto his tray and watched him walk off.

"ooo Alex, I think somebody likes you." I said and everyone at the table laughed.

--

I was at my locker after school and guess who came up to me. Yup, Luis. He had a brownish, purple circle surrounding his eye. A result of Ben's powerful punch.

"Lizzy.." He said.

I cut him off, "I don't think It's a good idea to be seen talking to me. Ben or Cameron will be angry. I'm sure you don't want a repeat of Saturday night from Ben.

He laughed. "So do you really go out with that white boy?" He asked.

"His name is Ben." I said with the worst attitude. "And yes I do."

"What does he have that I don't have, mamacita?"

"He respects me." I said and smiled at that thought. I glanced down the hall and saw Ben coming. The moment he saw Luis standing in front of me his pace quickened and before I could warn Luis, Luis had already taken off. I laughed to myself.

When Ben got a few feet from me he asked, "What did he want?"

I smiled, "Nothing. Nothing at all." I kissed Ben and took his arm "Let's get out of here."

Chapter15

B en's POV (finally)

"Stop." She said sternly but struggled to keep that beautiful smile off her caramel brown face. "I mean it, stop. I won't get anything done if you keep this up."

I chuckled and continued tracing kisses along her jaw line. All these months I resisted the urge to kiss her and hold her in my arms, now that I have the chance I will not take it for granted. Lizzy looked so cute while she was trying to concentrate on her math homework. The way her eyebrows would furrow as she studied the unit circle made me smile.

"Just one last kiss and I'll leave you alone." I said leaning my face close to hers.

She held her pencil still in her hand after listening to my request. "Fine." As soon as her lips touched mines, I deepened the kiss. I expected Lizzy to pull away from me because I didn't specify what kind of kiss I meant, but I heard her let go of her pencil and put her hands on my shoulders. I wrapped my arms around her. Our lips moved in sync and I didn't want the kiss to end.

After we were both breathless, we parted. I gazed into Lizzy's Chocolate brown eyes and said, "I'll let you finish your work...for now." I winked and she laughed.

"I think Cameron is in his room." She said picking up her pencil again and proceeding with her trigonometry homework. "He's probably feeling neglected by the fact that you are even in here with me instead of him."

"Alright." I got up and headed towards Cameron's room. The door was slightly closed, but I opened it anyway. It was a bad idea because Cameron and Taylor were in there doing exactly what Lizzy and I were just doing in her room a few minutes ago. He definitely didn't care that I was with Lizzy. So much for neglect.

I cleared my throat to make my presence known, but they still were going at it. I tried clearing my throat again and this time they stopped and looked in my direction.

"Dude, How long have you been standing there?" Cameron asked.

"Long enough to know that I have seen way too much." I said.

"Oops, sorry." Taylor giggled and her cheeks flushed.

I chuckled and shook my head, "No problem."

"I should probably go start my homework." Taylor says while sliding off Cameron's bed.

"Lizzy's in her room doing hers; You might as well go in there and join her." I said.

"Will do." She says walking quickly past me out of the room.

"She's cute when she's embarrassed, right?" Cameron says looking after Taylor as she walked out of the room.

I just shrugged and took a seat at Cameron's desk. "I need advice." I said randomly.

Cameron just stared at me. "On what?"

I ran my fingers through my hair and sighed. "Lizzy....me and Lizzy...us. She's uncomfortable when we are out in public and I guess I can't blame her, but I don't want her feeling that way.

Cameron nodded. "You have to understand something about my sister, Ben and about this town. You and I may not see a big deal with interracial dating, but they do. Lizzy senses that. Even when you two were not together, she still faced discrimination."

"I just wish it all stopped. I wish there was something I could do to change things." I started fidgeting with a pencil on his desk.

"Go out."

I looked up at Cameron. "To where?"

He just shrugged. "I don't know. Go grab something to eat. Show her that you don't care what other people think. Let her know she can be herself with you."

I pondered on his suggestion, and marched back over to Lizzy's room. The door was halfway open so I just peeked my head in. Her and Taylor were listening to music and talking while doing homework. They looked up at me when they saw me, but then looked back down.

"Hey Lizzy, wanna go out and grab a bite to eat?"

Without even looking up at me she said "no thanks." I was stunned.

Lizzy POV

"Uh, why not?" Ben asked awkwardly. I really did not want to go out and deal with people anymore today, but I didn't want to tell Ben this. "Aren't you hungry?"

I still could not bring myself to look at him. "I am a little, but there's food in the kitchen. I can make us something." I patiently waited for Ben's response, when I finally looked I noticed that he was gone.

"What was that all about?" Taylor said while sitting up.

I rubbed my face in frustration, "I'm not sure."

"Ben looked a little annoyed. Why didn't you want to go out?" She asked.

"I have so much homework to do." I lied.

Taylor's jaw dropped. "No you do not! Are you really that scared to go out in public with him?!" She screeched.

"Shh!!" I stood up and began to pace around my room. "No."

"Yeah!"

"No!"

"Lizzy, you don't know how good you've got it. Ben adores you. He is not ashamed to have you so quit being selfish and let him love you and show you off before some white brunette bimbo steals him away!"

"Taylor, you just described yourself." I chuckled.

She had a thoughtful look on her face, "did i? Well whatever! I would steal him but you know Cameron is my man."

I nodded, "uh huh."

"Listen, just be happy. Ben cares about you Lizzy."

I sighed. "Alright." I walked down the hall to Cameron's room and put on a smile. "I changed my mind, Ben, I'm starting to crave Panda Express."

Ben's POV

I carried a tray of Lizzy and Me's food to a table. I was so relieved when she agreed to go out to eat. I was trying every way possible to take her mind off of the stares, but I couldn't. They were too obvious. We started eating in silence.

I thought of something random for us to talk about. "So Ryan is totally obsessed with Pretty Little Liars now." Dumb convo, I know, but I could not think of anything else.

Lizzy just forced a fake laugh. I sighed and reached across the table and took her hand and rubbed it gently. "Lizzy, I just want to make you happy. Please let me."

She gazed at me and gave me a crooked smile. "Aw, Ben I want to make you happy too, but I don't know if.. I can." She said uncomfortably.

I let go of her hand. "What do you mean?"

She began to fidget with the food on her plate. "I..I'm not white, obviously, and you have already been getting a lot of crap for even being seen with me. Things are not going to be the same for you, Ben. You have a good reputation and you're popular and good looking. Do you really want to risk all that to be with me?"

I couldn't help but smile at her. "Liz, all those things mean nothing to me now. It's no one else's business who I date. If loving you is a crime then someone can come arrest me now."

Lizzy raised her eyebrows at me in surprise. "You love me?"

I actually did not realize I said that. It was probably too soon to start using that term, but I know I definitely have strong feelings for Lizzy. "Well, Lizzy, yeah. I do care about you a lot. I don't want to scare you away by using that word, though."

A smile appeared on her beautiful face. "That word doesn't scare me, Ben." She lifted a piece of orange chicken to her mouth and chewed quickly before saying, "I'm sorry for being so shy and weird and awkward. I'll try my best to not let what people say get to me."

"That's my girl. I know words hurt, but just know that we are going to overcome it all okay? Trust me on this." I said confidently, but still wondered how. It was definitely going to be a challenge, but its worth the fight.

LIZZY POV

Two months later, my relationship with Ben has been absolutely amazing. He is such a great guy with so much love to offer me. Unfortunately, the racial slurs have only increased. I really really tried so hard to pretend like it didn't bother me, but it did! So much!

It was Friday afternoon, I was so happy this week was over. I was up in my room just browsing on my phone and decided I was hungry. I went downstairs to find something to snack on. I heard voices in the kitchen I went in to find out what was going on.

My mom, Luke, Cameron, and Mckenna were all standing around.

"Oh wonderful, I was just about to call you to come down Lizzy. I have something to tell you kids." My mom said excitedly. I looked at Cameron in confusion and he just shrugged. He was just as confused as I was. My mom grabbed Luke's arm.

"Did you want to tell them, Luke? Or should I?" My mom asked him. I got this uneasy feeling at the pit of my stomach. "Oh I'll just go ahead and say it! Luke and I are getting married!" My mom beamed and put her hand in front of her face, revealing the ring on her finger.

At that moment i felt so sick, so empty. I couldn't even speak. I turned and ran up the stairs into my room and closed my door. I lay on my bed and cried silently with tears falling. I was feeling sad and frustrated at the same time. I then realized that Ben would be here any minute, we were suppose to go out tonight. I completely forgot. I quickly jumped off my bed, wiping my face with the back of my hand and sniffling. I didn't want to be upset while i was out with him. Being with Ben will make me forget about all of this.

I chose something casual but cute to wear and I heard the door bell ring. I quickly pulled my hair back into a low pony tail and exited my room. My mom had opened the door and was greeting Ben. She turned around and saw me and had a concerned expression and whispered to me.

"What happened, i look away once and your gone." She said referring to me leaving after she informed us of her marriage.

"I remembered I had to get ready." I lied. "Sorry" I felt anger rise again. "I have to go, Ben is waiting." I said walking past her to ben. I kind of shoved him out the door and slammed the front door as hard as i Could.

Ben took my arm. "Lizzy is everything ok?" He asked.

"Yeah, everything is fine." I lied again. I gave him a quick peck on the lips. "Let's go."

The car ride it was unusually silent. Ben and i always had something to talk about. He finally broke the silence by asking me, "are you sure everything's alright?" he glanced at me once then back at the road.

"mhm" i said staring straight ahead.

"im worried about you lizzy." he said and looked at me one more time.

i turned my head and looked at him, "dont worry ben, i'm okay" I paused. "everything is great." i reached to turn on the radio and nicki minaj blared and i sang along with it. "My anaconda don't. My anaconda don't. My anaconda don't want none unless you got buns hun." I began to sing along and dance at the same time in my seat. This made ben look at me and laugh.

"Somebody's in a dancing mood, I see." Ben said jokingly. "It doesn't distract me from the fact that something is still bothering you, though." I stopped dancing abruptly and rolled my eyes at him. Why can he read me so well? "I didn't mean to kill your vibe, Lizzy. I saw Luke's car in the driveway. Did he say something to piss you off today?"

"I hate Luke." I said through clenched teeth.

Ben slowed down at a red light. "Hate is a strong word."

"I know. That's exactly why I used it." I said. Ben chuckled. "They are getting married, Ben." Ben's jaw dropped. Even when the light turned green he didn't move the car. People honked loudly behind us. "Ben, go" I pointed ahead.

He released his foot off the brake and proceeded. "Wow...really? Geez, I don't even know what to say, Lizzy. I'm so sorry."

"Don't be its not your fault." I said. "Let's just enjoy tonight okay?" Ben took my left hand and kissed it.

"I'll always be here for you, Lizzy."

Chapter 16

Ben and I went to dinner and movie. It was nice to spend time with him, but the thought of Luke being a part my family made me cringe. It was 11 o clock and we were in Ben's driveway. Luckily he lives across the street and I can basically go home at any time.

"Want to hang inside for a bit? My mom hasn't seen you in 3 days, she misses you." Ben smiled. His parents were so welcoming to me. They treated me so well, regardless of my skin color and that made me feel so good inside.

I followed Ben inside his house. His mom and dad were sitting in the den watching a tv show.

"Hi Mr. and Mrs. Campbell" I waved.

Ben's mom got up and hugged me tight. "Hi Lizzy dear, how are you? Did you guys have a nice time out?"

I laughed. "We did. I'm fine and how are you both doing?"

"We are good!" Mr. Campbell said.

"We'll be up in my room if you need me." Ben said taking my hand. We went up the stairs.

"Your parents are so cute." I said.

Ben laughed. "They are, aren't they?"

I had been to Ben's room a few times before, but today it looked a little different. "Did you do something with your room?" I asked while looking around.

"Yeah I rearranged some stuff around. Do you like it?"

"It looks a lot more spacious like this. I like it." I said while plopping down on the edge of his bed and kicking my shoes off. I watched him closely as he took off his jacket and draped on his desk chair. Ben was so unbelievably cute! I am so happy I can stare all I want now without feeling nervous.

"Want me to put in a movie for us to watch?" He asked.

I shook my head no and laughed. "We just came from a movie, Ben. I just feel like cuddling."

"I like that idea way better." He said while smiling and walking towards me. I scooted over and made room for him. He wrapped his arms around me and kissed me sweetly as we lay next to eachother. Ben nibbled gently at my bottom lip. Then He made his way down to my neck and planted soft kisses. His kisses drove me insane! Each kiss was filled with love. His hands caressed my back while I ran my fingers over his biceps. I can't get enough of those.

We stopped for a moment and stared into eachother's eyes. "Can you do me a favor?" Ben asked with a serious face.

"Yeah,what is it?" I asked.

He smiled. "Can you just stop being beautiful for a second?" I buried my face in the pillow feeling slightly shy. I felt Ben run his fingers through my hair.

I looked up at him and said, "Can you stop giving me butterflies in my stomach for a second? Or nah?"

We both started laughing hysterically, when we finally calmed down I rested my head on his chest and listened to his heartbeat. It was slightly fast due to our laughter. He rubbed my arm gently. "Have you decided when you're going to go see Jaden again?" He asked.

"I thought about it, but I haven't really decided when." I sighed "My mind has been consumed with thoughts of having Luke inhabit my life. I don't know what to do."

"Maybe you should talk to your mom. Let her know how you feel about Luke."

"I would feel selfish...this is her chance at being happy again after her divorce. I don't want to ruin it."

"Lizzy, you can't let your mother marry a jerk. It will be hard for her accept it at first, but you should try to show her some proof so it doesn't seem like you're just making things up."

I bit my bottom lip. That was an excellent idea. I was going to have to prove how ignorant Luke really was and make my mother see it for herself.

--

The next day I stayed home from school because I woke up with a massive headache and just felt really tired and basically I just wasn't in the mood to deal with nonsense. I was binging on Netflix most of the morning while I was home alone and then I heard the doorbell ring. I rolled my eyes. Who would be coming here at this time? I heard it ring again, but I made no attempts to answer it.

I groaned and got up out of bed and made my way to my window to see if I could see whose car was in the driveway. I didn't see a car. Then my phone started to ring and I noticed Ben was calling me.

"Shouldn't he be in class?" I mumbled to myself as I answered his call. "Hey"

"Hey, babe. I'm at your front door. Would you mind coming down?" He chuckled.

"Oh, I'm sorry I'll be down in a second!" I hurried down the stairs and opened the front door and saw Ben standing there holding chocolate, a couple papers, and a DVD in his hand. I smiled "What are you doing here? You should be at school."

I let him in and he smiled "I knew you were not feeling good and I missed you at school today of course. I grabbed your homework and assignments from your teachers too" He handed me the stack of papers.

I reached and gave him a kiss "You're literally the best, babe. Let's go eat these chocolates and pop this DVD in"

We settled on the couch. "How are you feeling?" Ben asked me.

I wrap my arms around him "Much better now that you're here" Ben kissed the side of my forehead and gently caressed my arms as we watched Pitch Perfect and laughed at all the funny parts.

I heard Ben take a deep breath and sigh and say "Lizzy..I have something to tell you." As soon as he said that my heart dropped. I was starting to feel sick again.

I sat up and looked at him trying to study his face "What is it, Ben?"

He paused and he seemed nervous, "Lizzy..I love you" Ben said. I didn't even know how to react. "I'm not saying this to hear it back from you. I'm saying it to make sure you know."

I breathed a sigh of relief that it was not anything bad and my heart warmed up. I smiled at him at looked deeply into his eyes, cupped the sides of his face and planted a kiss on his lips and said, "I love you, too"

--

Ben's POV

Lizzy telling me she loved me back was amazing. I was nervous and thought it might push her away, but it actually has brought us closer. I loved spending time with her in any circumstance. Regardless of the stares we get in public I didn't care and I could tell Lizzy was also trying very hard not to, but I knew deep down it still bothered her so much. I wish I could take away the hurt and the pain, but I just did not know how to.

The following day I was standing by Lizzy's locker waiting for her after class. As I stood there I was on my phone scrolling when I noticed someone stop abruptly in front of me and stare at me. I looked up and saw Erin standing in front of me with an annoyed expression on her face.

"Ben." She said

"What?" I snapped.

"Why are you just standing here?"

"I am waiting for my girlfriend obviously" I said looking back down at my phone.

"How much longer are you going to do this act? Leave poor Lizzy alone she doesn't need your fake love." Erin rolled her eyes. My anger suddenly increased

"Erin, you need to get out of my face. Walk away" I said angrily. "Just because we didn't last doesn't mean our relationship is anything like mine and Lizzy's.

"Didn't know you liked black girls" Erin smirked "I would tanned myself a little more then"

"That's it." I shoved Erin out of my way and stood in the middle of the hallway. "Hello fellow students! Hope you all are having a wonderful day today! I have a public service announcement!" Everyone In the hallway stopped moving and talking and I noticed Lizzy in the distance staring at me confused. "I know you all remember how I dated Erin Maguire, right? Such an unfortunate mistake, I wish I could take back. In that time being with her I learned a lot..I learned that she stuffs socks in her bra to make her boobs look bigger! Oh! Implants weren't an option for her because she was too flat chested! So tragic, you all probably thought her boobs were enormous but sorry to break it to you fellas and girls who admired her."

I turned to see Erin's face bright red with her jaw wide open.

"Cotton breasts!!" Some guy yelled at Erin and the entire hallway erupted into laughter.

I walked past Erin and patted her on the shoulder and laughed "I warned you. If you said anything about Lizzy, I was gonna tell everyone your little secret" She scoffed and walked away briskly down the hall way.

Lizzy walked up to me with her eyes bright and wide "Ben! You were so cruel! I loved it!"

I wrapped my arms around her waist "I don't think Erin will be bothering you anymore"

--

Lizzy's POV

Ben just totally exposed Erin in front of everyone and it was the best moment ever! I couldn't thank Ben enough.

At lunch, Erin sat a table by herself because her plastic friends disowned her. She seemed so powerless without her puppets.

One enemy of progress down, and a million more to go.

I was in my room after school doing my homework when I heard voices downstairs. I opened my door and listened and heard my mom and Luke talking for a couple minutes and then I heard the front door close.

My mom and Luke went out together to I have no idea where, but I went down to see if anyone else was downstairs. I scanned the kitchen and realized I was home alone. I noticed Luke's briefcase on the ground against the couch in the living room. I eyed it suspiciously for a moment and then of course me being me, I went toward it. I crouched down in front of it and carefully opened it.

Since he was a lawyer, all I found were folders filled with papers regarding his cases. As I was reading a letter he had from the courthouse. Suddenly, a hand grabbed my shoulder. I jumped and screamed.

"Woah, hey it's just me." I whipped my head around and saw Ben standing behind me.

I breathed a sigh of relief that it was not Luke who found me looking through his things. I was so focused I hadn't even heard him come in. I brought my hand to my chest. "You scared the crap out of me, Ben." My heart was racing.

He knelt down next to me and rubbed my back and kissed the side of my head. "Sorry, Liz, I didn't mean to, and the door was unlocked." He looked at the papers I had in my hand. "What are you doing?"

"I'm snooping." I said as I continued to read. "This is Luke's briefcase and I'm determined to find something. Anything to end this relationship."

"Didn't I tell you to talk to your mom? And when I said find proof, I didn't mean do all this" Ben said pointing to the briefcase confused as to why I was going through all this trouble.

"Ben, I can't just go to her and say 'oh hey mom you can't marry Luke because I do not like him'" I said as I continued sifting through sheets of documents. "What other proof could there be?"

"Lizzy, stop." He brushed his over my arm. "Just tell your mom how you really feel. Even if it is that simple, which it's not. It is way deeper than that. He has racist tendencies."

"I know Ben, but...I" The sound of the front door opening interrupted me. I froze and began stuffing the papers back in the bag from panic. Ben rose to his feet and looked down the hall

"Relax, it's Cameron and Taylor." Ben told me. "Just tell her." I sighed in defeat and put the rest on the papers back into his briefcase.

"What's up you guys?" Cameron asked walking over to the fridge and grabbing two Pepsis, one for him and one for Taylor.

"Not much." I said nonchalantly.

"Are you kidding? Ben literally tore Erin apart today!" Taylor said excitedly. "No guy will date her, ever!"

I remembered and hugged Ben tightly "What can I say?" Ben shrugged. "I was provoked" We all started laughing.

"They... call her Cotton ....Breast now" I said giggling like crazy. It's hilarious.

Cameron chuckled "It's Friday night, you two got any plans?"

Ben and I exchanged a glance. "No, not really, why what's up?" I asked.

"Well there's this party..."Cameron began

"Oh God No" I quickly cut him off. After what happened at the last party I was done with parties.

"Okay I know the last party we went to didn't end so well, but this party will be EPIC I guarantee it" Cameron said.

Ben crossed his arms over his chest "How do you know?"

"One of the quarterbacks on the Football team, his name is Matthew or something. Super chill and I heard Erin has even been uninvited after her little ordeal today" Cameron ran his fingers through his blonde hair.

I stared at him "That proves nothing, you moron" I rolled my eyes.

"Oh come on it'll be fun! Won't be like the last party we went to, things have changed" Taylor smiled and gazed at Cameron lovingly.

"Well, I'm not going unless Lizzy is comfortable with going" Ben said gently rubbing my shoulder. I definitely did not want to be a party pooper and maybe Taylor was right, it may be different considering the circumstance right now. I am dating Ben and nothing Luis related would happen to me if we are together at all times. But then my mind wandered to the stares Ben and I would get while trying to have fun. I shook those thoughts away.

I can't let them stop me from having fun.

I looked up at Ben, "Yeah we should go." I said

"Are you sure? We really don't have to if you don't want to. We could watch a movie at my place or even just go out and do something" He said.

"It's fine really. Maybe it'll be fun." I shrugged. I hoped so.

Chapter 17

This party is so lame. I thought to myself. Ben and I were sitting there waiting for it to get fun and we were also people watching. Taylor and Cameron went off somewhere probably dancing. I would dance, but this music was just horrible and was killing my vibe.

"I can't take this horrendous music anymore!" I shouted at Ben even though he was next to me. It was so loud. I got up and went to the DJ and requested that he play a dub step remixed song. Something upbeat to get me going. He did as I requested and as soon as he played it people stood there confused. I didn't care though. I went to the dancefloor and started dancing by myself as everyone watched in amazement. Moving my body to the beat, I was having fun in my own world dancing.

Before I knew it there was a huge circle forming around me. I saw Ben standing in the circle watching me and smiling. Then he started cheering for me. I heard some people say "Wow, she's good. She can dance"

Next thing I know Ben came in the middle in started dancing with me. I did not even realize he could dance. He was pretty good. Whoever said white people don't have rhythm hasn't met Ben. For a moment it felt like no body was watching us and it was just me and him. The song ended and

I stopped dancing breathlessly and Ben gave me a quick peck on the lips. Everyone at the party clapped and cheered for us. In that moment I felt really good about my self and about my and Ben.

"You dance so well! Can you teach my girlfriend!" Some dude yelled and Ben and I laughed.

The DJ then played a different dance mix and I got right back into dancing and this time, everyone else started dancing too! They seemed to like the music even though I didn't think it would be music they would be in to. Every got back to dancing and having fun. I turned around and started dancing on Ben as he put his hands on my hips.

I eventually got tired from all that dancing and Ben and I walked off the dance floor. "Babe let's go get you hydrated" He said laughing "The way you move your body, Lizzy. Damn you can dance"

I started laughing. "You surprised me too. I didn't know you had moves like that." We found bottled water and drank it quickly. A girl walked past me and said, "Girl, I admire you. I wish I could dance like that!"

"Thank you" I smiled. This night was going better than I expected. I forgot about all the stereotypes"

BEN'S POV

Lizzy totally changed the game. When she started dancing in the center I was more than proud to call her mine. Beauty, brains, can sing and she can move her body to any rhythm. She was flawless! Seeing her so happy tonight made me incredibly happy.

"Ben, I am surprisingly enjoying myself." Lizzy said breathlessly after she gulped her entire bottle of water. "That was fun!" I was ecstatic that she was having fun.

"Did you want to leave now?" I chuckled.

"Leave? We are just getting started." She grab my arm and started pulling me back towards the dancefloor, "Round two is up next!"

--

The next morning I slept in. Last night's party was great. Thoughts of Lizzy and I dancing and not having a care in the world filled my mind. The way things should be everyday.

I got out of bed, quickly showered, and threw on a flannel button up and ripped jeans. Lizzy and I were going out for breakfast to Ihop. Lizzy looked beautiful as usual. We walked into Ihop hand in hand and Lizzy seemed to be in a great mood. As the waiter seated us at a booth, I noticed some elderly white couple sitting at a table nearby staring intently at us. I silently prayed that Lizzy wouldn't notice, but at this point I think Lizzy can feel stares as if they were daggers in her back.

I quickly brought up a conversation to divert her attention. "There's so many different options do you know what you're getting?" I asked her as we both scanned the menu.

She looked closely at the menu and briefly eyed the elderly couple a few feet away and quickly back at her menu. I really thought this was weird. Lizzy is a fighter, and last night she came out of her comfort zone, but right now something was off in her demeanor. This obviously isn't the first time we have had stares.

"I think I'll get an omelet, not sure about the sides yet." She said quietly. What is with her?

"Lizzy..are you..." I began to ask.

She cut me off and said quietly without looking up from the menu, "Look, I am trying very hard to bite my tongue. I do not want to go off on old people. It may lead them to cardiac arrest. I am just keeping it all inside for now so I don't explode and be that black girl with a temper problem. I do not want to cause a scene."

What she said wasn't funny, but I could not help but laugh anyway. My laughter made the couple look at us suspiciously. And I just nodded at them and said "Hi, How are you doing?" They quickly looked away.

The waiter came back and took our orders after bringing us our juice. Lizzy sat there stiffly looking as if she was trying so hard to contain herself. "Lizzy, if you want to blow off some steam you can go outside for a minute.." I said uncertain.

Lizzy chuckled, "Steam? I have fire inside of me right now." She suddenly slid out of the booth and walked towards the ladies restroom. I deeply sighed in frustration.

LIZZYS POV

I should be used to stares by now..I really should be. I just didn't want to offend the poor old folks. I have some morals, you know. I went to the restroom and just stared at my face in the mirror. The melanin on my face.

"What the fuck, dude. What the actual fuckin fuck." I said outloud. "It is the 21st century and race is still an issue. I can't enjoy a meal with my damn boyfriend without being gawked at." My anger was slowly slipping out and I felt a lump in my throat. I felt like crying. "Pull yourself together, Lizzy" I told myself. I refused to be broken.

I waited until my eyes were less red and I dabbed at my tears. Hopefully Ben won't notice I just nearly had a breakdown in the bathroom. All this was really getting to me .Last night was great, but right now I felt horrible. I felt worse for Ben, actually. He doesn't need to deal with this.

As I approached our table I noticed Ben talking with the elderly couple. I was confused. I made my way to my seat and forced a smile as I walked by.

"Lizzy, I was just talking to these lovely people. They wanted to know more about us and our relationship." Ben said with a smirk on his face.

"Huh?" I said terribly confused.

The old lady spoke up. "I was just astounded by how beautiful you are. I love your skin color and you two are just a beautiful couple." She said

"My wife really admires you two. Couldn't stop staring." Her husband said.

"Oh.." I said surprised "Well, thank you" At that moment the waiter brought our food. Ben and I began to eat.

"Are you feeling a bit better? It was just a misunderstanding, you know? I just asked if they had an issue and turns out they didn't. Just intrigued." Ben was saying.

"Ben, shut up." I snapped.

"What did I do?" He asked, his face filled with utter confusion.

I cut a piece of my omelet with the side of my fork and brought it to my mouth. "If you think someone is admirably beautiful, you tell them right? You don't stare at them. Staring is rude." I said annoyed.

Ben sighed heavily. "I know it is, babe. I know that staring is rude."

"Do you know what happened to me in that bathroom? I was talking to myself. Talking to nobody and swearing at nobody." I said and Ben just stared at me as if he was judging me hard. "Stop looking at me, staring is rude."

--

BEN'S POV

I am convinced Lizzy is crazy.

On the ride home she was talking about how things would be if she were white and to be honest it was beginning to irritate me. It was ridiculous.

"Like let's say we went to the mall, no one would have to follow me around because you know I wouldn't be black." She was saying crazy things all the way to her house. I went in up to her room with her and listened to the crazy things she was saying without saying anything in response.

"Are you mad or something? Why aren't you saying anything?" She asked as she unzipped her jacket and took off her boots. I sat on her bed just watching her closely. She came and stood in front of me. "I can't do this to you." She said in a monotone voice.

"What?" I asked not understanding what she was talking about. She was saying a lot of things that did not make sense anymore.

"People are always going to stare!" She exclaimed.

"Lizzy, why do you care what people think?" I said trying to keep my voice calm.

"Ben you are white. You are privileged. You have no idea what I go through on a daily basis or how I feel."

Those words stung. "I am always with you! Of course I know what it feels like!"

"You're white! Of course I care what people think, because it matters to me! That's the problem! I am ruining you!" She walked away from me and I was stunned at what she was saying. "Ben, you shouldn't even be with me. Us getting together was just a bad idea."

I stood up to my feet. "Are you seriously wanting to throw away our relationship because of what some prejudice people think?!"

"Yes!" Lizzy yelled.

--

LIZZY POV

I do not know what came over me, but I was filled with so much anger and pain that I didn't want Ben to go through this anymore. Being in my life made things between us complicated and I just took out all my frustrations out. As soon as I said the last word Ben briskly walked to my bedroom door and stormed out.

What have I done?

Chapter 18

It was Monday and I was walking to school. I was walking pretty fast because I didn't want to run into Ben and wanted to avoid basically everyone. I hadn't spoken to Ben since our heated argument Saturday after he stormed out of my room. So many thoughts were going through my mind. I felt so empty, but I had to keep reminding myself that Ben would be better off without me ruining his life.

As soon as I got to school I heard a couple of whispers and excited talk about how I killed it at the party Friday night, but I was sad that Ben wasn't with me.

I went to my locker and quickly took the books I needed out. I had my first class with Ben and I was prepared for the awkwardness.

I walked into class and people were chatty and were complimenting me some more about my dancing. I just forced a smile and said "Thanks." I saw Ben sitting at his desk and we made eye contact. I hurried to sit down without looking at him for the entire class period. This hour long class truly felt like an eternity. I just kept looking at the clock praying for it to end. As soon as the bell rang I was first the leave the classroom.

This was way more painful than I expected it to be. I longed to talk to Ben and longed for his kisses but I had to push those feelings aside.

Lunch was pretty awkward, well on Ben's part. I tried to act as normal as possible so the others wouldn't notice any tension between Ben and I, but Ben didn't even speak once which was unusual for him.

"Hey what's with you, man?" Cameron asked Ben.

Ben just shrugged, "Oh, nothing"

"You sure?" Taylor asked him and looked at me for answers.

"Yeah." Ben said and forced a chuckle "I'm just tired. Didn't get much sleep last night" and at that moment Ben looked me dead in the eyes accusingly. I felt my heart ache.

After lunch there were crowds of people and Taylor took that opportunity to ask me "Okay, what the hell did you do to Ben, Lizzy?"

I sighed, "We kind of got into a fight this weekend." I began to fidget with my hair.

Taylor's jaw dropped "What? No way! Things were perfect on Friday. Did you guys break up?"

"I don't really know honestly..i think we did. It's my fault" I said and explained what happened.

We made our way through the hallway and to Taylor's locker so she could put some things in it "Seriously Lizzy, you made a mistake. If he wasn't willing to be with you, he wouldn't."

"Taylor, it's just really complicated."

"So you're just not going to speak to eachother for the rest of your lives?" She asked

"I don't know." I said annoyed and glanced down the hallway. I saw Ben and Erin talking and my heart sunk. Ben's back was toward me and he had his shoulder up against a locker and she was standing in front of him smiling. What were they talking about? Why would she be smiling after he exposed her just a few days ago. Why did I feel so jealous right now? It hurt so much.

"You don't even act like you care." Taylor snapped.

"If only you knew."

--

The next day was just as painful if not more than yesterday. My mind began to circulate thoughts of Ben and Erin together. I saw Ben in my first period class and we didn't speak. He was also in my class before lunch, but for some reason he didn't show up. I wondered where he was. Maybe he will come in late.

I kept watching the door waiting for him to walk through but he never did. I figured he just ditched class and would show up to lunch. As I made my way to the cafeteria I saw Cameron.

"Hey." I said. "Have you seen Ben?"

Cameron looked at me funny "You didn't hear?"

"Hear what?" Concern washed over me.

"He got into a fight and got suspended."

"Wow what an idiot. Who did he fight and why?" I said shaking my head.

"He fought some guy, I don't know his name, but he said something about you and Ben completely lost it and started pounding on him."

My eyes widened. "Oh no.."

"That 'idiot' loves you. Stop making things complicated and quit being selfish." With that being said Cameron walked away and left me to think. I knew what I had to do next.

BEN'S POV

I don't know what it was, but Lizzy really seemed to be pretty calm about our whole fight and just us not being together at all. It hurt like hell. She just pushed me away because of what other people think and I do not understand it all. On Monday, we had to walk past eachother as if we were strangers and to see Lizzy all smiling and laughing as if nothing were wrong made me feel pathetic.

It was Tuesday and during my 3rd period class this guy decided to really piss me off. I already have been in a bad mood and he thought it was a good idea to provoke me. I was sitting at my desk minding my own business when the guy leaned over and asked me why I didn't walk Lizzy to class today.

"Where's your little chocolate pudding? She's hot. If I were you I would love to grab.." I cut him off. My anger reached it breaking point. I pushed him to the ground and started punching him. The sound of desks falling over filled the room. He clawed at my face and I continued go at it. A few seconds later I felt myself being pulled away by security guards and down to the dean's office.

I'm suspended for 1 week. I really didn't care. No one talks about Lizzy like that, whether we are on good terms or not.

I angrily walked out to the parking lot, threw my backpack in the back seat of my car and sped home. I went to the kitchen to grab something to eat since it was lunch time. I peered into the fridge and took some leftover dinner from last night and heated it up in the microwave.

I angrily chewed my food as I was seated at the kitchen table. I looked at my phone and saw texts from people asking about the fight I got into earlier. I ignored them all, I wasn't in the mood to talk about it. Then I heard the doorbell ring. That also agitated me. I grumbled and quickly walked to the door.

I opened it and was surprised to see Lizzy standing in front of me.

LIZZY'S POV

I walked quickly to Ben's house. I decided that ditching class wouldn't be so terrible since Ben is suspended. I was stupid for letting him go and for pushing him away. I was also pretty nervous. I didn't know what Ben would say or how he would react .

I found myself standing in front of his door for about 5 minutes just preparing myself and rehearsing what I would say. With a trembling hand, I pressed my finger on the doorbell and waited. I heard loud footsteps come towards the door and Ben opened it and stared at me.

"What, Lizzy?" Ben said sounded frustration.

"You got into a fight, Ben" I said. "You got into a fight and now you're suspended, and it's all because of me."

"I don't care that I'm suspended" Ben said flatly.

"Can I..can I please come inside?" I asked hesitantly and Ben moved aside so I could come in. I followed him into the kitchen and saw a plate of food. "Oh you're eating.."

"Why are you here? I know you didn't come to talk about me eating." Ben snapped.

I thought about what I rehearsed and I just lost it all from memory and broke down crying. I, Lizzy West was crying uncontrollably at this point.

"I...I'm....sorry...I" I couldn't even form a complete sentence. I had to turn away from Ben because I hated people seeing me cry.

I felt Ben come up from behind me and stand in front of me. He pulled me into a tight hug, "Shh..." He said softly. "Lizzy, stop. Don't cry." After a few minutes I was finally able to calm down. I was wiping my tears with the sleeve of my jacket. Ben was also using his thumb and wiping the tears off my face. He went and got me a box of Kleenex.

"I'm so...stupid" I said. Ben motioned for us to sit in the living room.

"You're not stupid. Don't call yourself that." Ben said.

"I really messed up. I truly thought your life would be better without me. It hurts so much. I love you more than I even realized and I was so selfish to push you away. You didn't deserve that at all ,Ben and I am so sorry." I said.

"You really didn't seem bothered." Ben said.

"Trust me. I was so bothered. I just covered it up." I admitted. "Please Ben, I don't care what others think. I just know that I want to be with you."

Ben stared at me and I watched as his hard expression softened. "Are you sure?"

I cupped his face in my hand and leaned in to kiss him. We kissed deeply and then parted and I said, "Ben, yes I'm sooo sure."

His dark brown eyes stared into mine and a smile crept onto his lips. Oh, did I miss that smile. "Tell me more." He said.

I laughed and smiled and kissed him again. "I am so sorry." He ran his hand through my hair affectionately. "It's just..so much going on. My mom and Luke, you and Erin."

"Woah, wait me and Erin? What about me and Erin?" Ben asked confused.

"I saw you guys yesterday..in the hallway talking and she was smiling so I figured..."

"Are you kidding? Erin? Never. She was only smiling because she noticed that we weren't talking and that made her happy so she was throwing it in my face." Ben explained and I was relieved.

I sighed deeply and Ben gently rubbed my back. "About your mom and Luke..." He began.

I cut him off, "I'll tell her. I really will, when the time is right." Another lump started to fill my throat and tears were streaming down my face. "I.. just don't want my family to..fall apart again, Ben. It's already hard enough being the only black person in my family. You can't understand racism unless you've experienced it for yourself. It really sucks. Feeling like everyone is judging you and looking at you like you're some sort of disease or any different because of the color of your skin." I looked at Ben and noticed in his features that he was really listening to me and taking in every word. His eyebrows furrowed in deep thought.

"Babe, I am so sorry for not being as understanding as I should have been. You really are unhappy here."

"Ben, you are like the main reason why I can find the strength to go out in public. I am black. I am a black female. My hair is curly and coiled. My skin is darker..."

"And I love it and I love you. Everything about you is beautiful." Ben stated. "We will overcome this, baby girl. You are so much stronger than you think"

--

Later that evening my mom called me and told me to start making dinner because Luke was coming over. Ew. She was running late coming home from work. We were having stir fry so I took out the vegetables and chicken from the freezer. As I was setting every thing out I heard the doorbell ring. Cameron was upstairs blasting some music so I knew he didn't hear it.

I went to answer the door and behold, annoying Luke was here.

"Oh, You're early...there is like legit no food ready." I said as a rolled my eyes and let him inside.

Luke chuckled. "I know. I finished work early so here I am."

"Oh Lovely." I said quietly and made my way back into the kitchen contemplating on whether or not to add bleach into his food.

I was going at it at the stove getting the food ready and I heard Luke sit down at the kitchen table. I didn't bother to turn around or even have a conversation with him. Of course, he started one though.

"So, Lizzy...what do you think you want to do with your life in the future?" I heard Luke ask. I rolled my eyes.

"Maybe deal some drugs...or even better, be a stripper. Heard they make that money." I said casually as I added some teriyaki sauce to the frying pan and stirred.

Luke cleared his throat, "Are you trying to be funny, Lizzy?"

"Do you hear me laughing?"

He chuckled, "I know you don't like me very much."

"Oh, did I make it too obvious? Oops" I said still with my back to him. I pulled my phone out of my pocket to check the time. Mom should be here soon. I can't stand being here with Luke.

"Listen to me, I am not racist." Luke said and I knew right then and there if he had to say that then he must be racist!!!! I went to my iphone's voice recording app, pressed record, and set my phone on the counter next to me.

"Who said you were racist?" I asked. "You already sound guilty."

"I just have different beliefs and opinions, which I am entitled to. I am a lawyer and you know how many cases there are with black criminals? A ton. Your mom probably didn't know what she was getting herself into when she adopted you. She might as well cut you off right now." Luke said.

"Oh really? Does my mother know that that's how you feel? If she doesn't, I can be glad to let her know"

He laughed, "As if she will believe I told you this. I am marrying your mom whether you like it or not so just get used to me. Hopefully in a few years I can convince her to disown you too."

I wasn't angry. In fact I was extremely happy, because I got all that he said on my voice recorder.

Finally I can end this engagement once and for all.

Chapter 19

I was done making dinner and mom still wasn't home yet. I left Luke sitting in the kitchen while I went upstairs to find my brother, Cameron. I reached the door of his bedroom and heard loud sounds of Eminem blasting from his room. He was seriously obsessed with Eminem. I pounded on the door loudly before opening it.Cameron was sitting at his desk working on his laptop and turned to look at me when I walked in.

"Hey, what's up." He said as he drew his attention back to his laptop screen.

"Luke's downstairs." I said as I plopped onto his bed.

"Really?"

"Yeah." I scrolled through my phone to my voice recordings. "Can you turn your music down , I want you to listen to something, Cameron." He did as I asked and I played the recording. The sound of Luke's voice on my phone played. I watched Cameron's facial features intently. He was staring hard at my phone and listening closely.

When the recording finished, Cameron stood up quickly, "I am going to kill that man." He walked briskly out of the room and started down the stairs. I ran after him.

"Cameron,no! Stop! You can't kill him!" I tried to grab his arm but he obviously was stronger than I. "Woah calm your tits, just wait a minute!" I yelled and he stopped half way down the stairs.

"Why, Lizzy?!" He exclaimed. At that moment I heard my mom's voice downstairs in the kitchen. I pondered for a second, "Actually..." I shrugged. "Get his ass."

Cameron didn't hesitate as he confidently walked down stairs. I followed closely behind Cameron as he stormed into the kitchen. Luke and my mom were engrossed in conversation. She was wearing a business suit and was playing with her shoulder length dirty blonde hair.

"So you really are a racist jerk aren't you?" Cameron said. My mom had a confused look on her face and Luke had a smirk on his face.

"Cameron, what on earth are you talking about? What has gotten into you?" My mom said as her eyes got wide.

Cameron got in Luke's face at this point. He hovered over him as he was still sitting at the kitchen table with a glass of water in front of him. "I am not going to let you sit here and disrespect my sister anymore. And I sure as Hell am not letting you marry my mother." Cameron said loudly.

"I don't know what your sister told you, but it's probably not true."

"Are you calling her a Liar?!" Cameron yelled. The last time I saw him this angry was when dad was caught cheating on mom. Exposing Luke like this wasn't exactly my plan, but it felt great to see Cameron standing up for me.

"What is going on here?! Lizzy and Cameron explain to me what you're talking about right now." My mom stepped in between Cameron and Luke.

My brother grabbed my phone out of my hand and played the recording "...I can convince her to disown you too" After the recording finished playing Luke had a stunned expression on his face and my mom had her hand over her mouth and her eyes were wide with shock.

"I...I..listen to me, Katherine, it's not what it seems." Luke said to my mother. "Recording me without my consent is also a felony."

"Then sue me!"I said as I waved my arms in the air. "Oh, but wait I don't think you will still be a lawyer after this gets to your law firm." I grinned at him.

"Looks like you lost your Job, and your Fiancé" Cameron said and pointed towards the door. "Please see yourself out."

Luke stood up and tried to talk to my mom. "Katherine..Katherine." He reached to touch her.

"Don't touch me, Luke! Get out of my house! I don't want to ever see you again!" My mom shoved him away. "You disgust me! Just go!" She was pushing him towards the front door now. Luke finally gave up trying to talk to my mom and left. It felt like a huge relief. My mother slammed the front door and stormed back into the kitchen. Cameron and I stood by the window making sure Luke actually left. His white Chevy Cruze backed up out of our driveway and down the street. Good Riddance.

"What do we do now..?" I asked him quietly.

"Give her some time." He said as he turned to walk towards the staircase.

"Cameron," I began and I went and gave him a tight hug and he returned the tight hug with an even tighter hug. "That was honestly the most savage thing I have ever seen you do in a long time.

Cameron chuckled. "I'm sorry, I haven't been the best big brother lately. I promise that will change. I wouldn't care if your skin was green with yellow polka dots. You are my sister and I love you."

I pulled away and smiled at him. "I love you too, Cam. You're the best brother ever." Cameron smiled back at me and turned and jogged up the stairs, leaving me standing in the foyer soaking everything in. I felt conflicted and did not want to face mom right now. I knew she must be devastated. I instead I went outside to sit on the swinging bench on the front porch. I glanced over at Taylor's House next door and then at Ben's across the street. He was in his garage playing with a soccer ball. Using his time being suspended wisely I guess.

He had no idea I was just watching him. I just watched this beautiful white human being who loved me dearly. Playing with a soccer ball...it made me realize how much I loved him. I loved Ben.

I glanced up at the sky and noticed the sun beginning to set .My thoughts were interrupted as I saw someone approaching me from the corner of my eye. Ben jogged over across the street holding his soccer ball in his hand and grinning at me.

"Hey, how long have you been sitting out here?" He asked breathlessly.

I smiled a slid over on the bench so he could have a seat. "Not too long."

Ben sat next to me and placed his ball on the ground in front of him between his feet and leaned forward, resting his arms on his thighs. "Everything okay?" I then took that moment to lean onto Ben and wrap my arm around his torso. "Aw what's the matter? Talk to me, Lizzy."

I sighed. "He's gone, Ben. Luke is gone for good. I would be jumping for joy all over the place but my mom is in the house bawling her eyes out."

His eyes got wide and he smirked. "No way. What happened?" I went on my phone and played the recording for him to hear. Ben's smirk disappeared and his expression turned serious. He shook his head in disapproval. "When will it end?" He sighed. "Racism..It really sickens me, Lizzy. You have no idea. "

I took a deep breath. "There are moments where it hurts, and then there are moments where you're just numb to it." I said. "I feel bad for my mom. I can't even face her right now. She must be so heartbroken. I just wish...." My words were cut off by my little sister, Mckenna coming outside.

"Lizzy! I need help." She said and Ben and I chuckled.

I moved my arm from Ben's torso and sat up straight. "What's up, Kenna?" I looked at her. She had a piece of paper in her hand.

"Time to do some homework." She said eagerly." Hi Ben!" If only I was this eager about my school work. My mom usually assigned Mckenna math problems, just to get her ready for school whenever she starts. She would be ahead. She is extremely smart and it was my job to help her get her problems done. Well I didn't get paid, but I didn't mind.

"Alright." I flipped through her little workbook.

"Luke made mommy and you sad and made Cam mad?" She asked randomly. I didn't even know how to answer, and I was caught off guard by her question. She was too young to even realize the things I go through on a daily basis.

"Uh, he just..had to leave." I said awkwardly and gave Ben a panicked look.

"What he say?" She asked.

I quickly changed the subject, "Okay you're working on addition problems today." I looked at her paper.

"Sorry Luke made you sad, Lizzy. I still love you sissy!" She patted my arm affectionately and that eased all the mixed feelings I had.

I smiled at how mature my 4 year old sister already was. I gave her a little hug, "Thank you Mckenna, I love you too."

"Awwww" Ben said dramatically and smiled at us. "You two are adorable." I hit him playfully.

--

Ben's POV

Seeing the way Mckenna loved her sister made my heart happy. My thoughts lingered on her mother sitting inside the house. I wondered what thoughts were going through her head.

"I can go in and check on your mom." I said as Lizzy began to patiently help her little sister with her math problems.

Lizzy looked up at me. "Are you sure you want to do that?"

I shrugged. "Sure. All I know is she shouldn't be alone right now." Lizzy gave me a weak smile and nodded that told me she understood. I rubbed and patted her thigh before standing up and walking inside the house.

Lizzy's mom was seated in the living room sipping wine and staring at a blank television screen. I just sat down next to her without saying a word.

There was a long silence before she finally spoke. "I remember the day I brought Lizzy home." She said and took a sip of her wine and smiled to herself. "She wouldn't say a word, but I knew that she was happy to finally have a family. We would hear her crying softly at night. I thought maybe she was unhappy. I went into her room and noticed she was in fetal position with her hands on her ribs. She would cry by herself when she was in pain."

Lizzy's mom sighed and continued, "Her dad and I asked her to tell us what hurt, and she said her chest had been hurting her for months but her foster mother just ignored it. I took her to the doctor the next morning and they said her ribs didn't heal properly after they broke in the accident and so now it would effect her since she didn't come in sooner. This innocent child in pain and no one in the foster care system did anything about it." She shook her head.

My thoughts went to Lizzy. How I wanted to hold her closer to me in that moment. No one should have had to go through what she went through, especially as a child. I can't even imagine. It just makes me want to show her more and more love. I remembered how I was so carefree as a kid, and here Lizzy was grieving the loss of her parents and not knowing where her brother was, and having physical pain. It was unimaginable.

"She has always been so strong." She smiled now. "This beautiful black little girl was going to be raised by a white family. This beautiful, smart, and sassy little girl was my daughter now. My ex husband and I would do anything for her, to protect her and keep her safe to make sure she's happy." She picked up a picture of Lizzy and Cameron off the coffee table which looked like a picture from their first day of school probably almost 10 years ago.

" Cameron was so excited about having a sister. He was always there to protect her and he showed it today. How could I not see that this man I wanted to marry was racist? I should have known when he thought my daughter was my maid. How could I have missed it?"

I saw Lizzy walk up and lean against the wall and I noticed her face was filled with empathy for her mom. She had her arms across her chest and was staring down at the ground and listening. I saw tears stream down her face and she quickly tried wiping them away.

"She loved singing and dancing." Her mom chuckled. "Honestly, she got the whole family into dancing as well. I cant' even imaging my life without Lizzy. She made our family complete." Tears streamed down her face

There was a silence. And Lizzy emerged from the corner. "Mom..?" She said with tears in her eyes. I was expecting her to say something sweet and comforting, but instead she said. "Why are you acting like I died?" She said partially laughing through her tears and wiping her face with the tips of her fingers.

I couldn't help but chuckle and her mom chuckled as well. "Oh sweetie." She sniffled. "I just..I let you down.

Lizzy came and sat on the other side of the couch and embraced her mother in a tight hug. "Mom, you are my mother. You adopted me and provided me with the best life. Better than I even dreamed of. You never let me down. And I know that my parents are looking down on me happily knowing that I was raised by such a wonderful family. You and dad have given me more than I even thought I was going to have. I love you so so much mommy."

"Honey, I love you more" Her mom rubbed her back affectionately and kissed her forehead.

I nearly lost my cool and was about to start sobbing. I was able to contain myself and only one tear escaped my eye. This moment was beautiful. I did not see a black girl and her white adoptive mother. I simple saw a mother and daughter who deeply cared for one another, which was beautiful. I only wished that everyone saw things in this way.

Lizzy and her mom pulled away from eachother with tears in their eyes. Lizzy laughed softly as she wiped her face and looked at her mom. "Remember when I threw a butter knife at Cameron when we were younger though?"

"A steak knife." Cameron walked into the room smiling but his eyes were a little red, which also meant he was a little emotional as well after hearing his mother and sisters interaction. "It was a steak knife, Lizzy. You threw a steak knife at me." All of us burst out into laughter.

"Well I don't know about you all but I am starving." Lizzy's mom stood up and went into the kitchen "And you really made that racist asshole food too? Lizzy you are an angel." She said.

"Learned it from you, momma." Lizzy chuckled.

"I knew I must have done something right." Her mom smiled as she got a plate of food and poured herself some wine "I'll be in my room if you kids need me." She disappeared down the hallway.

"I'm hungry too. I'll make us all a plate of food." Lizzy got up and went into the kitchen, leaving Cameron and I in the living room.

"She really is an angel." I said with many thoughts running through my head.

"Did you forget she attacked me with a steak knife or..?" Cameron said and we both laughed. "To be honest, my sister has been through so much. Don't get me wrong, she's really strong, but at the same time, she is sensitive.

"I am not sensitive!" Lizzy shouted from the kitchen.

Cameron scoffed and whispered. "I know her better than she knows herself." He stood up and went into the kitchen. "Thanks, Lizzy." He got his plate of food. "I'll eat upstairs, I have to call Taylor."

"Seriously?" Lizzy said as she stared at her brother and then looked over at me. "Will you eat with me atleast?"

I smiled at her. "Of course. Just give me a minute." I just needed a minute to gather my thoughts and my emotions.

Lizzy walked over to the couch where I was seated, sat on my lap, and wrapped her arm around my neck. "What's the matter?" My response to that was giving her a tight hug and kissing her softly.

"You're amazing. I hope you know that." I said as I gazed into her dark brown eyes. She smiled at me and played with my hair affectionately.

"No, Ben, you're amazing. I am beyond lucky to have a guy as caring as you in my life. Thank you for being you and thank you for always having my back. I really don't know what I would do without you." She said. "I love you." She kissed me deeply.

--

Lizzy's POV

Three weeks had passed since my life had been Luke-free. My mom was dealing with it well and my life had gotten better. My relationship with Ben had probably been the best it had been in a while and that was because I was learning to disregard everyone else's opinions.

Today was the day progress reports would be given out and everyone was feeling anxious. They were being handed out during our last period class of the day. Mine was Chemistry. My teacher went around the room passing each student their progress report and when I finally got mine the teacher said to me.

"See me after class, Lizzy." Mr. Johnson said. The whole class got quiet and stared at me, including Erin Maguire who laughed, but thought better than to say anything to me.

I flipped over my progress report and looked at my grades. I had straight A's. I wasn't really surprised in all honesty. I mean to say this in the most humble way possible. So when Mr. Johnson said he wanted to talk to me the first thing that I assumed he was gonna say was that he thought I cheated my way to these grades. I would have to wait until the end of class to find out.

As soon as the bell rang and everyone filed out of the classroom I went up to the teacher's desk

"Lizzy..." He began. "You have the highest grade in the class right now." I stared at him waiting for him to say something insulting. "I think you need to start tutoring your peers." He said and I was actually not expecting that.

"Huh?" I said confused.

He smiled at me. "You are a very bright student, Lizzy and I have a student who has been really struggling in the class. She is failing right now."

"Oh, that sucks."

"Erin could really use some tutoring, and I think your help would be great for her."

A volcano literally exploded in my head. Erin Maguire. The same person who was laughing at me for getting called to talk to the teacher after class like I was stupid is the person who is actually stupid.

"Um, I think I'll pass, Mr. Johnson." I said as I shifted my weight from my right leg to my left and readjusted my backpack strap on my shoulder uncomfortably."

"If you tutor her, I will excuse you from the final exam."

"When do I start?" I asked desperately. I had good grades, but I would never pass up an offer to be excused from an exam. I hate taking tests more than I hate Erin.

Mr. Johnson smiled. "Will tomorrow after school be good for you?"

"Sounds good." I said.

Let's see how this goes.

I walked out of class and saw that Ben, Taylor, Cameron, Ryan and Kevin were in the hallway by Ben's locker looking at eachother's progress reports.

"Hey, what took you so long?" Taylor asked as I approached them.

"Mr. Johnson just wanted to talk to me." I said.

"Let me see your progress report." Cameron said reaching for mine and handing me his. "Lizzy how the Hell are you and Ben so damn smart. You both have straight A's."

I looked at Ben and saw him smiling at me and I smiled back. I knew he was smart, but he just didn't like to show it.

"Ben you literally ditch class every day. How do you get straight A's?" Kevin exclaimed.

"And Lizzy you're always falling asleep in class how do you do this?" Taylor whined.

I just shrugged and laughed. Ben came and put his arm around me. "Atleast I am present in class while I'm sleeping." I teased.

Ben laughed. "Hey it doesn't matter how you get the job done as long as you get it done."

I looked at Cameron's grades. "You have straight C's mom is going murder you."

Cameron snatched it from me . "I have one B, don't you see it." We all started laughing.

Taylor abruptly stopped laughing and we all turned down the hallway to see Erin walking by us. She saw us and rolled her eyes at us. Tutoring her tomorrow was definitely going to be a challenge but I was ready for it.

Chapter 20

"You know you don't have to do this, right?" Ben said.

"I know." I replied.

Ben and I were walking down the hallway at school after our last class ended. He was walking me to the school library, where I was meeting up with Erin to tutor her. We reached the two large double doors to the entrance of the library and stopped. I peered through the rectangular windows on the door and spotted Erin sitting a table. She was applying red lip stick onto her lips while looking into a little compact mirror.

"That is not her shade." I said while shaking my head with my face pressed against the window.

Ben chuckled and pulled me away from the window. "Did you want me to wait for you?" Ben asked.

I sighed and said, "No, it's fine. Just go home. I can walk after I'm done."

"Okay." Ben looked at me intently. "Just don't accept any rides from strangers." I knew he was making a Luis reference and I hit him playfully.

"Ha. Ha. Funny." I rolled my eyes. "Get out of here."

Ben smirked at me, gave me a quick peck on the lips and watched me as I entered the library. As I approached Erin, I saw how horrible and bright that lipstick looked on her. It was definitely going to be a distraction. Who even thinks to apply lipstick before getting tutored?

As soon as I reached the table I slammed our Chemistry Text book on the table in front of Erin and she jumped. "Okay let's make this as smooth and painless as possible. I don't like you and you don't like me so we're even. I am only doing this because I don't want to take the final. I couldn't care less if you fail the class." I said plainly and her expression was filled with surprise and disgust and then she rolled her eyes. She literally had nothing to say back to me. I took a seat next to her.

I opened the text book to the chapter we were on in class. It was on calculating percentage yield from a limiting reactant. "Okay, let's just start by working on the homework problems." I said scanning the homework problems. "Actually, you need to first understand stoichiometry."

"What is stoichiometry?" She asked.

"It's like doing mass and mole conversions."

"Oh with avocados number,right?"

I stared at her blankly."His name is Avogadro."

"Whatever. So, how are we suppose to know the mass of the compounds or elements."

"There's this fancy thing that they give us on every exam in class. It's called a periodic table. Use it." I said flatly. My 4 year old sister was smarter than this chick. I took a deep breath and sighed. I silently prayed for patience, because I was lacking it at the moment.

I decided to go back 2 chapters and start with the basics. I explained everything that was necessary for her to understand percent yield and we did a couple of practice problems. The one hour session went by pretty quickly and I was happy about that. I could not stand to be in Erin's presence for longer than that.

"Is it making sense at all?" I asked as I started packing up my things into my bag.

"Yeah, it actually does." Erin replied, but rolled her eyes.

"Careful, your vision deteriorates with every eye roll." I said.

Erin looked at me with her blue eyes and scrunched her nose. "Oh, really?"

"Yeah, so stop." With that being said I walked out of the library laughing silently in my head. She is so gullible. I was actually looking forward to tutoring her tomorrow just to mess with her.

--

The next afternoon Erin and I met up at the same time and place. Going over homework problems and concepts that were foreign to her.

"Can we take a break." She whined. What a lazy cow. Her attention span is that of a toddler.

"We have only been here for 13 minutes." I said.

"That was still a lot."

"Just explain to me the concept of acids in conjugate pairs."

Erin sighed in frustration. "When the acid...that's H-A?" I nodded and she continued. "when it loses a proton it forms a base which is A minus and when that accepts a proton back again it reforms the acid H-A and that makes the two a conjugate pair."

"Exac-" I was cut off by the sound of a girl's voice.

"Erin? What are you doing here? With her.?" A girl with bleach blonde hair wearing an olive skirt with a white top was standing in front of our table. I had seen her around school a couple times, but I didn't even know her name.

Erin looked uncomfortable for a second. "Oh.. hey Sharon..we..well we were just studying together." She stuttered as she lied. Erin had mentioned to me before how she wanted to keep our sessions lowkey so people didn't know how dumb she was and how embarrassing it would be for her to be tutored, especially by a black person.

I spoke up. "Oh studying? That's what this is? Last time I checked you were failing chemistry and needed my help. I am not the one studying. You are. Don't get it twisted." I looked up at Sharon, and said "And next time, mind your own business." Sharon scoffed and turned and walked away.

"Wow, why are you such a-" Erin began and I cut her off.

"Stop complaining." I snapped.

"What does Ben even see in you?"

"Well, for one, I have actual boobs. Hm let's see I have a brain. I'm not a slut."

"I'm not a slut either."

"I have observed otherwise."

"Your brother Cameron wanted me so bad." She said and I nearly gagged.

"Yeah which explains why he's dating you right now, right? Oh..wait..." Erin shut up fast. "You try way too hard. Clearly guys know you're easy and take advantage of that." I said.

Erin looked down at the table and fidgeted with her pencil. "That's not true." She said quietly.

"You spread open your legs more than your textbooks..." I said and there was an awkward silence.

Erin began, "Ben....I really liked him, a lot. Seeing you two together now, I don't know. He just never looked at me the way he looks at you. He never kissed me the way he kisses you."

I was slightly disturbed at the fact that she even knows how Ben and I kiss. She really was pathetic. Being a hoe can't be that stressful.

"Do I look like a diary or a therapist to you?" I asked. "Quit telling me about your feelings."

Erin looked at me confused. "You're really mean."

"I know. I don't care. I also don't care about your sad love life and we will not talk about Ben or anyone else during tutoring. Got it?"

She sighed. "Whatever, fine."

She is so annoying.

--

I walked home from school and as I was passing Taylor's house saw her step mom unloading groceries out of her car. I already knew she didn't like me so I didn't acknowledge her, but the most surprising thing happened.

"Lizzy, right?" I heard the woman say. I ignored her and just kept walking because I didn't want any trouble and didn't want to have to curse her out.

"Wait, Lizzy." She repeated and I was halfway up my driveway but turned around to look at her. She was standing there looking at me. "I don't even know where to begin." She laughed nervously while setting a grocery bag on the ground. "

"I'll save you the trouble. Don't even start." I said.

"What I have done...what I've said to you, it's unforgiveable." She said. Her light brown hair blew crazily in the wind and she tucked strands of hair behind her ear.

"Go on." I encouraged.

"What I am trying to say is that I am a terrible person. For being racist towards you and for interfering with yours and Taylor's friendship." She said.

"Who hurt you?" I asked.

"What do you mean?"

"Why are you racist? Did some black person ever hurt you?"

"Well, no. I grew up in a little farm with my family. My parents were very conservative and I just had minimal contact with blacks. I just had this preconceived notion about you all. But you're different."

"I'm not different. I'm still black. We are still human beings and deserved to be treated as such. You are ignorant. You apologizing me doesn't change the fact that you are racist and you growing up on a filthy farm is not an excuse. I accept your apology, and never cared if you liked me or not. Taylor and I will be friends regardless of what you think of me." I said and turned to continue walking to my front door.

As soon as I walked into the house I saw Cameron and my mom standing at the window. Clearly watching the entire interaction I had with Taylor's mom.

"What did she say?" Cameron urged.

"If you told me she was rude to you, honey, I would gave her a piece of my mind sooner." My mom said.

I raised my eyebrows. "You talked to her?"

"Cameron told me everything. About what she said to you and about you and Taylor not able to be friends. As soon as I heard this we marched over next door and I told her off!" My mom exclaimed.

"I interjected occasionally. I couldn't go completely wild like I did with Luke. I am still dating the woman's step daughter." Cameron added.

I laughed. "Wow, you guys are straight savage." I fist bumped Cameron and hugged my mom.

"How was tutoring?" My mom asked.

"She is a dumb hoe. Literally and figuratively." I said.

"What's the word for 'hoe' again? Thot?" My mom began.

"Mom...please...don't..." I began.

"Hm.. rain drop, drop top, thot thot,."

"Noooo! Stop It, mom." Cameron said while covering his ears and walking away. I walked away too leaving my mother trying rap. We both ran up the stairs.

"Cookin it up in a crock pot. Bad and Bougie." My mom rapped as she strolled into the kitchen. Yup that is my mother for you.

When I got to my room I called Taylor and told her to come over because I wanted to gossip. She was sitting on my bed in less than 5 minutes. I loved having a friend that lived next door.

"She did whattt?" Taylor asked compeletely puzzled.

"She tried to apologize. It was a bad apology, but she tried."

"She is like bipolar, I swear." Taylor shook her head.

"Girl, Erin is bipolar too." I said. "She is disturbed on so many levels." I explained her whole transparent moment where she was heartbroken over Ben.

"That is definitely true. Ben and her were an odd couple. He is way in love with you than he ever was with her." She explained.

"She hated me way before Ben and I even started dating." I said.

Taylor plopped onto her stomach on my bed. "She is totally racist and jealous of you."

I sat my back rested against the headboard of my bed and raised my knees to my chest and looked at Taylor puzzled. "How can you be racist and jealous of someone that makes no sense?"

"You can sing, you can dance. You are like hotter than Beyonce'." Taylor said and I scoffed. "Girl your body is like a perfect 10. By the way, I need to know how your butt is so big and how you keep your stomach so flat."

I couldn't help but laugh hysterically. "Umm, I am no Beyonce' and I don't remember the last time I exercised because all I do is eat junk food."

"Anddd this is why all the girls at school hate you." Taylor said and we both laughed. I just shook my head. I watched as Taylor's expression turned serious. "Can I ask you a question, Lizzy?"

I was actually scared about her question and hesitantly said. "Sure..." White people ask strange questions sometimes.

"Can you like... teach me how to dance?" She asked.

I chuckled. "Oh definitely." I was excited because I LOVE to dance. I got up off my bed and got my phone off the dresser. I went on youtube to find a song. I played 'Release' by Timbaland. One of my all time favorite songs to dance and get loose to. I started dancing to the beat. "Alright, now you just move to the rhythm" I said to Taylor.

She stared at me as if I were speaking a foreign language from my bed. "I have no rhythm, Lizzy. I'm white."

I shook my head and danced over to her to make her get up. "Come on, it's not that bad. I promise. Even though you're white." I smiled. She got up and I held her hands to move her to the beat to give her a feel for how to move her body.

"Oh goodness." She said.

"You're doing great." I laughed.

'Why didn't anybody tell you guys were having a dance party?" We turned and saw Cameron standing in the doorway.

"OH wow, this is embarrassing" Taylor said while still trying to dance.

Cameron joined us in the middle of room and began dancing as well. He already knows how to dance. My whole family does. The West family has got rhythm.

I let go of Taylor's hand. Letting my little white baby go and be free to dance on her own. She was really doing well! I was excited. Cameron and Taylor started dancing together now. I became a third wheel. I didn't care though and was dancing on my own until my mom and Mckenna came dancing in.

We all started laughing. My mom was savage when it came to dancing. Mckenna was also a dancing queen. I changed the song to 'Bamboo Banga' by M.i.a.

With my hands waving in the air I started singing along with the lyrics.

"This the bamboo banga I said bamboo banga This the bamboo banga I said bamboo banga And we're hittin our records like a tennis player"

"Bamboo banga bamboo banga bamboo banga" Mckenna sang happily as she danced around. The song ended we all were smiling and giggling. This was probably the most fun my family has had since we moved into this house. The only person missing out on this fun was Ben. I made a mental note that I needed to call him later.

"Guess what! Guess what!" Mckenna exclaimed.

"What?!" Me, Cameron, and Taylor asked.

"My birthday is in 3 days!"

"Woahhh!"We we all said excitedly.

"What are we doing for her birthday, Mom?" I asked.

"Well I was thinking of having a party here at the house on Saturday. She's invited her classmates from preschool. I'll need a few extra hands that day with cooking, decorating, games and arts and craft stuff. So you can let Ben know too." She ran her fingers through her dirty blonde hair. "I also need to order a cake. I am gonna go make a list. Thanks for letting me turn up with you teens." She said as she danced our of my room holding Mckenna's hand and we all laughed. My mom's wild side was coming out from hibernation and I loved it. It was great to see her happy again.

I sighed and turned to Taylor and Cameron. "K. I am gonna call Ben now. Stay if you want but I would prefer you to leave."

They both laughed. "Gladly." Cameron said.

I plopped onto my bed and called Ben. It rang and rang and went to voicemail. I wonder where he is. I called back again and there was no answer. Where is this guy?! I have things to tell him!

--

Ben's POV

My mom sent me to the grocery store because she wanted to make some salad for dinner. All the way to the store for some lettuce.

Seriously?

I was standing in the aisle where all the produce was and it was freezing. I saw so many different bags of salad and lettuce I was confused. I called my mom to verify which one to get and while I was on the phone with her I noticed Lizzy calling me. As soon as I was done talking to my mom I called Lizzy back.

It rang once and then she answered. "BEN!!" Lizzy screeched into the phone.

I chuckled. "Hey." I carried the proper bag of lettuce and was looking for a short check out line.

"Where are you?" She sounded annoyed.

"At the store. I had to grab something for my mom." I explained.

"Oh.."

"Everything okay?"

"I miss you and was worried about you. I have stuff to tell you!"

I was amused. "You what?" I asked teasingly.

"I MISS YOU. There are you happy?"

I laughed. "I am so happy." Lizzy has really opened up to me now compared to when we first started out relationship. It's hard for her to express her emotions sometimes and just really talk about her feelings. I know she feels a certain way but just can't being herself to say it outloud.

I found a short line and got behind this old lady. "Hey, Liz, I'll be over in like 20 minutes I just need to go take this lettuce to my mom. I'll see you later, okay?"

"Okay, see ya." She said. I waited for her to hang up the phone before I slid my phone in my back pocket. I patiently waited as the cashier, who looked like a biker dude with a ton of tattoos on his neck, rang up the old womans items. I noticed the candy on the side and grabbed two snickers bars. They were Lizzy's favorite.

When it was finally my turn the cashier jokingly said, "balanced diet, I see."His voice was husky as if he smoked regularly.

I chuckled and shook my head. "My girlfriend loves snickers. And my mom loves lettuce."

"Ooh girlfriend huh? You got a pic of her?" He asked curiously.

"I'm kind of in a hurry, my mom needs this let-"

"Oh come on. I wanna see the lucky girl."

I took out my phone and showed a selfie of Lizzy and I. I watched as the man's eyebrows raised in surprise. "That's her?"

"Yep, that's her. My beautiful girlfriend." I put my phone away.

"Hm..interesting. Your girlfriend is cute, but you would look better with a white girl"

"Your opinion doesn't matter. Just ring up my stuff and make the transaction." I said angrily.

He chuckled. "Woah, slow down. No need to get upset."

"Don't tell me who I look better with." I looked at his name tag that read Nick. Then I snatched the grocery bag and my change from him and walked past the old lady who was still trying to put her money away in front of me and left the store. On the way home I called the grocery store and asked to speak to the manager.

"Jonathan speaking."

"Jonathan, hey, I just left your store. One of you cashiers named Nick made a comment that I didn't..."

He cut me off. "Oh, that was you..this elderly woman came to me a couple minutes ago filing a complaint about an interaction she witnessed between one of our employees and a customer. I fired Nick on the spot." I was speechless I didn't even know what to say. What a sweet old Angel. "Hello? Are you still there?"

"Yeah, I'm here."

"I am so sorry about that. We do not tolerate that at our store. "

"No, no it's not your fault. Thank you for handling it." I said.

"Any thing else I can do for you?" Jonathan asked.

I slowed down my car and turned into my driveway. "No thanks so much." I hung up the phone feeling pleased that that idiot was fired, but still angry at the stupidity and prejudice in the minds of people. I went inside and gave my mom, who was in the kitchen, her lettuce and made my way to Lizzy's.

Her mom let me inside and I jogged up the stairs trying to shake off any visible anger. I heard music coming from Lizzy's room and her beautiful voice singing along. Her door was cracked open and I peeked inside. She was standing in front of her dresser and braiding her hair. She had one braid neatly done on one side of her head and she had just started the other side. I leaned against her doorframe unnoticed and listened to her sing:

"Bask in the glory Of all our problems 'Cause we got the kind of love It takes to solve 'em

Yeah, I got issues-"

"You do." I interrupted and she stopped singing abruptly and snapped her head in my direction. Lizzy rolled her eyes at me, smiled and shook her head at me and went back to braiding. I came up behind her, while she had both of her arms up and her hands slowly weaving between the 3 strands of hair. I placed her snickers on her dresser in front of her. Then, I wrapped my arms around her waist from behind and kissed her cheek softly.

I saw her gasp and smile in the mirror. "You're the best!" I just responded by giving her another kiss. "I'll be done in a minute." She said.

"Take your time." I said and walked over to her bed and made myself comfortable. "What stuff did you wanna tell me?" I asked curious.

"Erin is still in love with you." Lizzy began, "She totally creeps on us and how we kiss and interact. It's weird."

"Seriously? She told you all this?" I asked surprised.

"Yes, can you believe it?" Lizzy finally finished the braid, put some stuff on the front edge of her hair and turned around. "You like it? They are called goddess braids."

I smiled. "You look beautiful." Lizzy was really too cute.

Lizzy smiled at me. "Thank you, Benjamin."

"Anytime, Elizabeth." We liked to joke around with our full first names sometimes since we both hated being called by them.

She made her way to her bed next to me and we laid close together. "Ben?" She asked.

"Yes?"

"How long did you and Erin date?"

"Hmm...only for like 5 weeks. This was like our freshman year by the way. I didn't know what I was doing and had hit puberty."

"I mean but in those 5 weeks, she really fell in love."

"I don't know why, it was only 5 weeks.." I said.

Lizzy scoffed. "Boys.."

"What do you mean 'boys'?"

"It doesn't matter if you two dated for 5 minutes. It's enough time for us girls to get attached and fall in love and wreck ourselves." Lizzy explained and I pondered on it for a moment.

"Lizzy?"

"Yeah?"

"When did you start having feelings for me?"

"Honestly, I am not exactly sure, because I probably tried to suppress them. Yeah you were a jerk and I hated you when I first met you, but you were still so nice to me in a jerksishly kind of way.. " She said and I chuckled. "Everytime you touched me, I just felt...something. I don't know what it was. But, remember the day you came with me to see Jaden? Everyone thought you and I were dating and that's when I just sat and really looked at you and thought about it and realized I liked you. I also realized you were hot which made me embarrassed to be around you."

I legit started laughing so hard and Lizzy told me to shut up. "That explains why you started acting so weird and started avoiding me. I just thought I did something to make me uncomfortable. Well, I was attracted to you, because of how much you disliked me." I said.

"What? How does that work?" Lizzy asked confused.

"All girls swoon when I walk in a room, but you used to roll your eyes or gag." We both chuckled. "That was kind of hot. You were hands down beautiful, I realized from the moment I met you and heard your voice on the playground, but your mean attitude was hot." I paused unsure about if I should proceed to say what was on my mind. "Don't be mad if I tell you this."

"Tell me what?" She asked.

"Remember on the camping trip, how we got lost because I claimed to not know what a compass was? I was a boy scout, of course I know what a compass is." I said laughing.

Lizzy shot up and jumped off her bed so fast I was startled. She stood with her arms crossed over her chest. "You lied!?!?!? You almost got us killed by a bear because you thought it would be funny?!" She exclaimed.

"Oh stop being dramatic. Calm down." I said as I motioned for her to lay back down.

"I could kill you right now." She said through clenched teeth getting back onto the bed.

"But you love me." I kissed Lizzy even she was too annoyed to kiss me back. "That was the only time we got to spend together alone, and I was curious wanted to know more about you. Encountering a bear wasn't in my plans okay? It's a funny story to tell when we look back on it. You're strength was even more attractive to me. It gave me hope that no matter what comes my way, I can overcome it."

"Hm..I remember you saying that I give you hope." She said

"I never told you this before, Lizzy..."

Lizzy closed her eyes as if she were in pain and said, 'I got a glimpse of your journal in homeroom when we had to write something positive about our camping partners." My jaw dropped. I tried so hard to not let her see what I wrote.

"You are seriously a pain in the ass. That was private information." I said and mentally prepared myself for what I was going to say next. "The night Luis tried to rape you, I knew I didn't just have some attraction to you. The thought of him trying to take advantage of you made me angry more than anything. Literally every time I see him in the hallways until this day I want to just punch him in the face." Thinking about it made me angry too.

Lizzy affectionately touched the side of my face and rubbed her thumb gently over my cheek. "You were my hero that night. And you have been since you came into my life. Without you I wouldn't have found Jaden, and living here would be a total nightmare. I don't know what I would do without you, Ben. I love you so much. Moving here sucked, but you have made me so happy." She said. I hugged her and kissed her forehead.

"Being loved by you is truly a blessing." I said and it really was.

Chapter 21

Lizzy's POV

I groaned as I heard my phone's alarm go off. I rubbed my eyes and grabbed my phone off my nightstand. It was 5:45 in the morning on Saturday. I was exhausted. Did I mention it was 5:45 in the morning? I am not a morning person at all. I was taking my driving test today to get my drivers license, finally. I shut off my alarm and trudged over to the bathroom in the hallway. My eyes were still half closed so I accidently walked into the doorframe with a loud thud.

"Crap." I mumbled. Cameron was in the bathroom with his towel wrapped around his waist and was brushing his teeth. He was indeed a morning person. He would wake up an hour early to have breakfast and make himself look presentable. Me, on the other hand, I would rather get an extra hour of sleep than eat breakfast or care about how I looked.

I knew he just showered because his hair was wet and in all crazy directions on his head. He spit toothpaste out of his mouth and into the sink and said to me ,"Goodmorning."

"Yeah a good morning for you." I mumbled, still half asleep.

"Shower fast. We need to leave by 6:15. The DMV opens at 7 and it takes like 30 minutes to get there. We don't want to have to wait for a long time. We have to get back here to help mom set up for Mckenna's party." He explained while shutting off the faucet and placing his toothbrush in its proper holder.

I was leaned against the doorframe and just said. "Mhm." I waited for him to exit the bathroom so I could shower quickly.

It was 6:17 and Cameron and I were walking out the door. I was making my way to the passenger side of his BMW on the driveway.

"Um where are you going?" Cameron asked me while dangling his keys toward me. "You're driving, Lizzy."

"Cameron, noo" I whined. I really just wanted to take a nap. "I don't want to drive."

Cameron stared me in confusion. "Who doesn't drive to their driving test?"

"Me."

Cameron just shook his head and shoved his keys at me. "No, you are driving." He got into the passenger seat.

I sighed in annoyance. "If I fall asleep at the wheel and we die. That's on you." I said. I got into the driver's seat and started driving. I already knew how to drive pretty well. Cameron taught me how to drive a while back so I am pretty comfortable with it.

I got onto the expressway and was thankful there were barely any cars since it was still early on a Saturday. We made it to the DMV in perfect timing and did all the necessary paperwork. Cameron and I chatted a little in the car while waiting for the person who was supposed to give me the driving test.

An old woman with angry eyes emerged from the building and my heart sunk.

"Wow she looks intense." I said nervously.

"Yeah, she looks like she could fail somebody before they even move the car." Cameron said.

"Not helping." I said while rolling my eyes.

Cameron patted my shoulder. "You'll be fine. You know how to drive." He hopped out of the car. "Good Luck."

The old lady got into the passenger seat and I decided I should probably butter her up a bit.

I smiled big. "Goodmorning, how-"

She cut me off sounding disinterested in what I was saying. "Drive." She said flatly. I silently prayed that these 20 minutes would go by fast.

--

"How does it feel?" Cameron asked me.

"It just feels like I got my license." I said in a bored tone.

"You're no fun." Cameron said.

So yeah, I passed my test after enduring that cranky old lady. I was glad it was over and that I could drive legally now. Since we were out here I decided to stop by a beauty supply store nearby and get some hair. I wanted box braids. There was no beauty supply store near our house. When I realized we would no longer be living by one that was 5 minutes away but instead almost an hour, I was shook.

I drove about 20 minutes and reached the little strip mall with the beauty supply store. I was driving and suddenly Cameron yelled, "Lizzy, Stop!!"

I slammed on the brakes and we both jolted forward. There was a stop sign hidden behind a tree and I didn't see it or the car that was crossing in front of me. My heart was beating fast and I was a little shaken up. I turned my head to look at Cameron and gave him a weak smile, "Oopsies..." I said letting my foot off the brakes.

"You need to go give your license back." He said.

I found a parking spot and we both got out of the car. I saw people of different races all around us. "Cameron, do you see all this melanin? How refreshing is it?" I spun around in the street as if I were in a field of flowers. I missed seeing black people.

Cameron just chuckled. We walked in the store and I went to the back of the store where the hair I needed was. I was looking through the packs while Cameron was trying on hats and wigs of all sorts and checking himself in the mirror and constantly asking "How do I look?"

"You look ugly." I said without even actually looking at him and being engrossed in deciding what hair color to get.

"I am getting this hat. It makes me look so cool." He said totally unbothered by my insult. I looked up at him and just chuckled. He came up behind me and looked at the hair I was looking at. "So...are you going with the 1b and a mix of another color?" He asked. He has seen me do my hair a million times and knows which hair color I get and everything.

"Hm, I am debating." I said unsure.

A voice I didn't recognize startled my thoughts, "Ohhh, that is cute. You brought your man with you to shop for hair. And he knows his stuff. I need to get me a white boy too." A black woman, who I assumed was the owner of the store, who had long blue acrylic and eyebrows that looked like they were glued on rather than drawn on stood next to us.

"Um..." I began, but she cut me off.

"You are too cute honey." She said eyeing Cameron and I looked at him and his face was turning bright red. She chewed her gum rhythmically with her mouth open. This lady was probably atleast 25 years old.

"Uh, this is my brother, not my boyfriend." People have often mistaken Cameron and I for a couple at times or even just friends so this was nothing new to me.

"Hey brother." The woman waved and smiled enthusiastically and Cameron just nodded and smiled uncomfortably.

"I think I'll just have one color." I grabbed 6 packs of the 1b Expression brand quickly to remove myself from this woman's presence.

"Need help finding anything else?" The woman asked.

"No. I-" I backed up quickly and bumped into a row of wigs placed on Styrofoam heads. They fell to the floor. "S-sorry" I mumbled as I frantically put them all back into place. "I think we are ready to check out." I said.

I followed the woman and I heard Cameron laughing at my clumsiness as he walked behind me.

"Shut up, brother." I said in a fake cheery voice, mimicking the owner.

As the lady rung up our items she asked me, "Do you need a hair braider to do your hair? I know this African hair braiding salon not to far away from here." She explained as she typed away at her cash register.

My instant thoughts went to what I heard about African salons. I was told they braid really tight and snatch your edges off. I may be wrong but I have full edges and was not about to give them up. "No, I usually do it by myself." I said.

"Let someone else do it for you." Cameron said to me quietly. "It takes you hours. Nearly all day when you do it by yourself."

"It's expensive, Cameron." I whispered.

"Can't be that expensive at a salon." Cameron whispered as if he knew what he was talking about. "How much do they charge?" He asked the woman loudly.

"About two hundred dollars."

Cameron's eyes went wide and he looked at me in shock, then back at her. I already knew this so I gave him an 'I told you so' look. Then he said, "Yeah she's fine. She can do it by herself."

The woman just shrugged. "You know, you really remind me of Rhyon Brown. That actress. Your voice sounds a little like her too. " She said to me.

I forced a laughed. "Yeah, you are probably like the sixth person in my life who has told me that." It was true, I got that a lot.

"Can you sing like her too?"

"Nope." I took the bag of our things and quickly said "thanks."We walked, almost ran, out of the little store to the car.

"Two hundred dollars!? That is insane!" Cameron exclaimed in the car. I told him to drive, I wasn't in the mood anymore.

I looked at the time and it was 9 :30. When we got home, it was close to 10:30. We began setting up for Mckenna's birthday party. Cameron was with the guy setting up the bouncy house in the back yard, my mom was in the kitchen getting food ready, and I was decorating the foyer with banners and balloons. I was standing on a double sided ladder and was about 10 feet high above the ground in front of the front door, when someone from outside was opening it.

"Wai-wait!" I yelled as I began to panic. I tried to yell to whoever was on the other side, but they forcefully pushed it open, and this removed the ladder from under me and sent me falling.I closed my eyes bracing myself for the pain of a crushing my skull, but instead felt myself being caught.

"What the hell?..OH! FUUUU-" I heard Ben yell right before catching me. "I am so sorry I didn't know you were behind the door." My face was inches from the ground and my butt was in the air as his left arm caught me at the waist. I felt his left arm shaking uncontrollably as he tried to hold me up.

"Just put me down." I said. "Gently." I added. He did as he was told. I was now sitting on my knees taking deep breaths trying slow my heart that was beating insanely fast.

"Everything okay, Lizzy?" My mom shouted from the kitchen.

"Oh yeah! Everything's...fine!" I yelled back. I really should have made sure the front door was locked.

Ben helped me up and I wiped off and I smoothed out my pink and blue flannel shirt.

"Are you okay? " Ben asked with concern written all over his face.

I smiled. "I am fine. Luckily you caught me or I would have probably broke my face." I said. My hero saving me once again. I gave him a quick peck on the lips.

"Glad you didn't." He said rubbing my back. "Why are you the one doing this? Where's Cameron?"

"He's out in the back working the bouncy house. I'm almost done, actually." I said looking around the decorated foyer.

Just then a shirtless Mckenna was standing at the top of stairs yelling down at me. "Lizzy! I need help!" Ben and I chuckled.

"I'll finish it up okay?" Ben said to me. Cool with me. I was tired of almost losing my life today. First the stop sign and now falling off the ladder.

I went upstairs and followed Mckenna into her room. "I want to wear my princess dress." Mckenna said pointing to the poofy pink dress on her bed.

"No, Mckenna. We picked out your birthday outfit last night remember?" I said walking over to her mess of a bed with clothes everywhere. I searched in the pile of clothes and found the shorts and teal blue tank top. "Here it is." I said holding it out to her. "And you can wear your sandals. It's going to be nice outside."

Mckenna folded her arms over her chest. "No! It's my birthday and I don't want to wear that!"

I sighed and rolled my eyes in annoyance. She was being a real brat right now. "I don't have time for this, okay? Mckenna, put it on right now."

I tried to forcefully put the tank top over her head, but she just darted out of her room and screamed "NOOO" and I chased her down the hallway. She threw off the tank top so she was shirtless again. Mckenna ran into the bathroom and I knew she was going to try to lock the door. This was a given.

As soon as she ran into the bathroom and tried to slam the door, I tried to stop her from closing it. Lucky for me, she slammed the door on four of my fingers on my right hand and I screamed in pain. It hurt so bad.

"OWWWWW!!! MCKENNA I AM GOING TO KILL YOU!" I yelled really loudly. Then I heard Mckenna start crying. I held my 4 fingers with my left hand as if that was going to soothe the pain. It didn't.

"What is going on up there?" I heard my mom say from the kitchen and then I heard multiple footsteps running up the stairs. My mom, Ben, and Cameron appeared in front of me with concern and confusion on their faces.

"Mom, get your daughter." I said pointing to the bathroom and breathing fast . I need to really hit the gym or something. Chasing her was really a work out and I am out of shape. "I think she broke my fingers!" I put my hand out for them to see and my fingers were swollen and turning purple.

"Oh no..honey.." My mom said examining my fingers.

Ben came and held my right hand and asked, "Can you move your fingers?" I moved and wiggled my fingers, but grimaced in pain. "Okay, good. That's good, Lizzy. This means they aren't broken." He said assuringly.

"I'll get a an ice pack from the freezer." Cameron said. "It'll reduce the swelling." First, he went up to the bathroom door with Mckenna locked inside and said, "Mckenna! You hurt Lizzy. Come out and say sorry right now."

"She said she would kill me!" Mckenna screamed. "I don't want to die!"

My mom, Cameron, and Ben gave me a look that said really Lizzy?

Okay, fine I probably shouldn't have used those words. I just shrugged and mumbled ,"it slipped out."

Cameron sighed, "She's crying Mckenna. She's too injured to kill you. She didn't mean it." Cameron gave me a look and motioned with his hand for me to start crying.

I began to sob. Well, fake sob atleast, and then the bathroom door opened slowly and Mckenna emerged. She looked concerned about me and ran to hug me. "I'm sorry I didn't mean to hurt you, Lizzy."

I sighed. "I know." I said patting her back.

"I'll get her dressed. Can you kids just make sure everything is set downstairs? The little ones should be arriving soon. And Lizzy get some ice on those fingers and take some Tylenol." My mom said to us, and Ben, Cameron, and I nodded and did as we were told. It was like I had a death wish today.

I took some Tylenol to relive the pain and Cameron got me an icepack to put on my fingers. Ben held it in place for me, while Cameron went out to the backyard to make sure things were good to go with the bounce house.

"Is it feeling better?" Ben asked. We were standing in the kitchen.

"Yeah it is." I said. "Thank you Dr. Campbell. You're gonna be a great doctor one day." I smiled up at him.

He grinned at me and said ,"That means a lot coming from you. Thanks, Lizzy."He gently grabbed my chin and kissed me once and I don't know what happened, but we were full on making out while standing in the kitchen. I took the ice pack from hand and tossed it on the counter so I could wrap my arms around his neck and bring us closer together. He rubbed my back and grabbed my butt a couple of times.

Suddenly Mckenna ran into the kitchen and tried to squeeze between Ben and I. Ben and I stopped and looked down at her breathlessly and then up at eachother. Ben smirked and winked at me and couldn't help but laugh. That was his way of saying we could continue making out later.

Mckenna didn't even seem to realize what she interrupted because all she said was, "Lizzy! Braid my hair too. I want us to be twins!"

I still had my goddess braids in and knew what she meant. She really just wanted 2 french braids, but didn't realize the difference. I sighed and looked at Ben. "Appreciate those joyous moments you have as an only child" I told him.

I carefully split Mckenna's blonde hair into two sections and began braiding one. I was kind of struggling a bit actually. As I grabbed strands of hair and tried to weave them together they kept slipping from my grasp.

"Hm?" Ben said. "Having technical difficulties?" He said looking at Mckenna's hair and then back up at me.

"My fingers." I began. "They are numb from the ice pack."

"Ah.." Ben said understanding. He leaned back against fridge with his arms folded across his chest watching me struggle in frustration to braid my little sister's hair. I just kept trying anyway, took me way longer than it usually would have, but I was able to finish both sides and make little miss bratty pants happy.

"Alright, all done." I said

"Yay! We are twins now!" Mckenna skipped happily out of the kitchen and I just shook my head.

"You know she adores you, right?" Ben asked.

I took the ice pack off the counter and walked over to fridge, "Hard to tell when she is being a serious brat." I said as I tossed it back in the freezer.

I sighed, put my hands on my hips and turned to face Ben. "Where is Taylor?" I was talking more to myself, anyway.

Ben just shrugged and followed me out into the back yard. The huge bouncy house was set up, but Cameron was no where to be found.

"Are you thinking what I'm thinking?" Ben asked as we stood in front of the large blown up house.

"Oh, yes." I knew exactly what he was thinking because I was thinking the same thing. Bouncy houses were definitely more fun for teens than kids and I definitely wanted to have a chance before the little twats arrived.

Ben parted the entrance to the inside and stuck his head in, hesitated and groaned. "Seriously? You guys, the children will be here any minute could you keep it PG?"

I squeezed in next to Ben and peered inside. Cameron and Taylor were making out and totally ignored Ben's comment. Ben and I went inside anyway and started jumping around all over. This made Cameron and Taylor bump their foreheads together.

"Ouch." Taylor rubbed her forehead and sat up.

"You two are so disrespectful." Cameron said while holding his head and rolling off of Taylor. They both tried to stand up but Ben and I proceeded to jump right next to them, which made it difficult for them to stand so they kept falling over. Ben and I were laughing our heads off.

After Ben and I decided to stop being annoying, we stopped jumping so Taylor and Cameron could stand up. Taylor pointed behind me, 'Look, the little rugrats are here." I followed her gaze to the 15 kids, including Mckenna, running full speed to the bouncy house where we were.

Today should be interesting. I prayed silently for patience

--

BEN'S POV

It was like a freakin crayon box. There were kids of all races and ethnicities. Black, white , Indian, Hispanic, Arabic, you name it. All these kids happily playing together and completely colorblind. I only wished that they would remain color blind for the rest of their lives, but I knew society would manage to distort everything as they grew older.

Lizzy, Cameron, Taylor and I got out of the jump house as the little ones stood outside eagerly outside of it.

"I get to go in first!" Mckenna said excitedly.

"Why?" A boy with blonde hair and overalls asked.

"Because it's my birthday, duh." Mckenna said as she went in first. Talk about sassy. It was so funny it felt like déjà vu almost to me but I couldn't remember how.

Cameron stayed around the jump house to make sure no one got hurt while I tossd a beach ball with the kids who got bored from jumping already. Taylor was also out here in the backyard playing dress up. Kids were rather dressing her up. They threw gold beaded necklaces and a hat and scarves all over her .

"O-okay..I- I think that's enough for me now." She said frantically and I laughed silently in my head . Lizzy set out napkins and paper plates out on the rectangular wooden picnic table.

I brought my focus back to the kids I was playing with. Mckenna had joined us too by now.

"I need to pee pee!" The same little blonde kid who questioned Mckenna's authority earlier.

"Go tell my sister." Mckenna pointed at Lizzy who was now talking to Taylor.

The boy ran up to Taylor instead and told her. I mean it was an honest mistake right?

Lizzy held her hand out to the kid and said, "Here, I'll take you to the bathroom."

"Mckenna told me to ask her sister." He said pointing at Taylor and Taylor's eyes went wide.

Lizzy just rolled her eyes. "I'm her sister." She said with an annoyed tone.

"Yeah, I'm not Mckenna's sister." Taylor added with an uncomfortable expression on her face.

"But why don't you look like Mckenna?" He asked.

Mckenna heard his question too and yelled, "Are you blind, we have the same hair, see." She pointed to her head. "We are twins! She is my sister!" Mckenna screamed.

Taylor quickly spoke up, "Here, let's go to the bathroom. It's okay." I could tell she did not want things to escalate and did not want to be in that awkward situation any longer.

Lizzy rolled her eyes and mumbled, "Annoying child." She briskly walked back into the house and I brought my attention back to the children in front of me.

"That kid is so annoying. I don't know who invited him." Mckenna said while rolling her eyes. And I then it literally hit me. Mckenna was like a mini Lizzy. Just tiny and white instead. I don't care what biology says, they acted the same even though they had no blood relation at all. Mckenna was witty, and sassy just like her sister. Environment is just as important, if not more.

I laughed silently in my head. How did I not notice this before.

I tried to distract Mckenna by throwing the ball to her. "Lizzy is the best, right Mckenna?" I said.

Mckenna jumped up and down and yelled, "Yes! She is my favorite. I love my sissy!" She ran to get the ball.

"Hey what about me?!" Cameron yelled across the backyard.

Mckenna shrugged. "You're okay." She said with her enthusiasm dying.

I just about died of laughter.

Later, we all ate and had cake. It was around 6 when the last kid had left the house. We were all helping clean up everything when the doorbell of the West residence rang.

"Who could that be?" Lizzy asked while wiping down the counter. Her mom walked down the hall to get the door. Me, Lizzy, Cameron and Taylor exchanged confused glances when we only heard whispers down the hall.

Mrs. West came back into the kitchen smiling. "Mckenna, there is surprise here for you." Right after she said that, Mr. west, Lizzy, Cameron, and Mckenna's dad walked in.

"Daddy!" Mckenna ran and jumped into her arms.

The first person I looked at was Cameron, because I knew he hated his father with every fiber of his being.

"Get the fuck out of here." Cameron said loudly and everyone in the room was silent.

Okay, now this is awkward.

Hey everyone! Please comment. I love reading your comments. They really keep me going and help me to know that people are reading and enjoying my story. I am having mixed feelings about how I should end the story just because I love the characters so much. More to come soon! I'll try my best to get chapters out more quickly! THanks for reading!

Chapter 22

B en's POV

I have only met Lizzy's dad one time before this so I kind of forgot what he looked like. He really resembled Eric Dane to me. Cameron really needs to humble himself because if it weren't for his dad's good looks he got, he wouldn't have girls drooling over him.

You could feel the tension between Cameron and his dad, but his dad didn't seem to care much about what Cameron said.

"Hey sweetie. Happy birthday." He picked Mckenna up and kissed her cheek. "How was your party?"

"It was fantastic!" She said happily.

"Wow, fantastic? That's great." He put her down.

"Hey, dad" Lizzy smiled as she came and hugged him tightly. "I missed you. I didn't know you were coming."

He kissed Lizzy's forehead and said, "Yeah, I thought I would surprise my two princesses." He smiled at her and Mckenna. "I got you this for your birthday. I can't believe you're five now." He pointed at a hugely wrapped box next to him.

Mckenna eagerly tore the wrapping paper off which revealed what was underneath. "A Barbie dream house!" She exclaimed.

Mr. West turned to face Lizzy, "And I heard you got your driver's license today." He reached into his pocket and pulled out keys. I watched as panic ran across Lizzy's face.

"Dad..no, you didn't..no." She stuttered.

"Go check out your new car. It's outside." Lizzy took the keys slowly and looked back at Cameron as if waiting for him to explode. And just like clockwork ...5...4..3...2..1.

"You can't be serious." Cameron shook his head and walked out of the kitchen.

"Such a drama queen." Lizzy rolled her eyes and then focused her attention back at her dad. "Thank you thank you thank you!' She through her arms around his neck and hugged him tight.

"Anything for my princess. Now you and your friends go check it out."

We walked towards the door. Cameron was sitting on the stairs as we walked past.

"Come on, Cameron." Taylor urged while taking his arm.

"Um, he is not bringing his nasty attitude into my car right now." Lizzy said. Taylor stayed behind to talk to Cameron.

Lizzy's new car was really really nice. It was a 2017 brand new silver Lexus GS 350. I sat next Lizzy in the front. She was about to back out of the driveway when Taylor ran out side waving her hands.

"Wait for us!" She screamed. Cameron walked slowly behind her with a pissed expression on his face.

"I am seriously getting really angry. Cameron is doing the most right now." Lizzy said and shook her head, "Why is he like this." She said quietly.

Taylor and Cameron climbed into the back seat. "Oh, these seats are nice. I am loving this car, Lizzy. Your dad has good taste in cars." Taylor said.

Cameron, on the other hand, kept ranting about his dad. "He is ridiculous. Thinks just buying us stuff will make us forget everything. I hate him. He is just..." We all ignored him and sat in silence. After a few minutes of driving Lizzy put the volume of the radio on full blast, drowning out Cameron's voice

"Drug houses, lookin like Peru

Graduated, I was overdue

Pink Molly, I can barely move

Ask about me, I'm gon' bust a move"

Lizzy sang along as she kept driving.

"Um...where are you going?" I asked her, but she didn't hear me so I repeated myself a bit louder. "Lizzy."

She finally heard me speaking and said "Huh?" as she turned down the volume.

"I was asking where you're driving to." I said.

"Chipotle. I want a burrito bowl." She said nonchalantly. "You hungry?" She glanced at me and I shook my head. "Are you hungry, Taylor?" Lizzy raised her eyes to look through her rearview mirror at Taylor.

"I'm good." Taylor said.

"You're not gonna ask me?" Cameron's angry voice rose from the backseat. I turned in my seat to look back and Cameron and his face was red with anger.

"You look like a fuckin tomato right now. Get it together or just shut the fuck up." Lizzy snapped and then turned the volume back up on full blast.

When we finally returned home from Chipotle, their dad's car was still parked on the side of the street. Lizzy parked her car in the driveway. Cameron quickly got out of the car and slammed the door so hard the entire car shook.

Lizzy's jaw dropped. "Wait, did he just.." She looked at me stunned before rolling down her window and sticking her head out. "Have you lost your mind?! Who the hell do you think you are slamming my door like that?!" She yelled at Cameron who was walking up to the front door. He completely ignored her and kept walking.

"Oh man. I really don't even know how to handle him right now." Taylor said. "I've never seen him this mad before."

"Go kiss him. it'll make him feel better." I said jokingly.

"I already tried that earlier. It didn't work." Taylor said as she got out of the car and ran after Cameron.

Lizzy slowly got out of the car and I did the same. She stood next to her car. Her annoyed expression turned into a sad one. I walked around the front of the car to her. "What's wrong, Lizzy?"

She sighed and clutched her bag of chipotle close to her chest. "I had so much fun at Chuck E. Cheese on my fifth birthday. So much fun, I knew that I would remember that birthday forever. The only thing was, I didn't know it was going to be unforgettable really because it was the same day I lost my family. My parent's died on my fifth birthday and I will never forget that, Ben. My last birthday with them was when I turned five." Tears streamed down her face as she spoke angrily through clenched teeth. I wrapped my arms around her and rubbed her shoulder. "Today she turns five, too. Mckenna deserves to have a better end to her great birthday. I don't want her to remember it as a fantastic party and then her family being dysfunctional with her dad showing up and her brother going crazy."

"I understand you completely, Lizzy." I brushed my thumb across her face to wipe the tears away and I kissed her on the lips. "You are an amazing older sister to Mckenna. She is so lucky to have you. And you know what we are going to do? We are going to go inside and make sure her birthday stays fantastic. I don't care if I have to play with barbies to do it." I said.

Lizzy laughed and looked up at me. "Gosh, I love you."

"I love you more." I said as we walked inside the house. Taylor and Cameron were seated at the bay window. She looked like she was trying to calm him down. It must have worked because his face wasn't red anymore.

We stopped in front of them. "Lizzy, are you okay?" Taylor asked.

Concern washed over Cameron's face. "Were you crying? What's wrong? What happened?" Even though he was mad, he still cared.

"He cheated on mom, not you." Lizzy began. "Yeah, I know it's like he cheated on all of us. I know. But if mom can forgive him and be civil with him when he comes around, why can't you?" Lizzy sighed. "You think I forgive easily, but in reality I just know what it feels like to lose people you love without warning. If dad died today, Cameron, how would you feel? You would probably feel shitty and regret being so rude to him."

I looked at Cameron. His expression softened and he averted his gaze to the floor.

Lizzy continued. "He did a terrible thing to our family. I am not defending him. At some point he was there for us whenever we needed him to be. He was at all of your baseball games. Dad always was in the front row of my ballet recitals recording me. He has been a good father to us. You shouldn't forget that. Today of all days, can you just not show how mad you are? Just pretend you are happy, I don't really care. But I do care about Mckenna, because she is our little sister and we have to make sure she is happy too. Stop thinking this is all about you. It's not. Grow up, Cameron, seriously." Lizzy spun around on her heels and walked towards the kitchen and I heard her call out her sister's name and ask to see her dollhouse.

I crossed my arms over my chest and stared at Cameron. "You weren't the only one hurt by your dad. You need to let this go. He is always going to be your dad. You have 2 sisters who need you as that male figure now that your dad isn't around as much. If anything, do it for your sisters." With that being said I walked away to find Lizzy and Mckenna. I walked past their parents who were drinking wine in the kitchen.

Lizzy and Mckenna were in the living room and they were both giggling. Lizzy was laying on her stomach on the carpet while Mckenna sat on her knees. They wer e playing with barbies in the dream house.

"Hey ladies." I said as I sat down on the other side of Mckenna. "You having fun, Mckenna?

"Yes! Best birthday ever!" She said happily.

I heard footsteps approach from behind us. I turned to see Cameron and Taylor joining us.

"Take me on a tour of the dream house, Mckenna." Cameron said forcing a smile.

"Here is the Bedroom, this is where she...."Mckenna began and I was relieved that Cameron actually listened. I could only hope he would sort things out with his dad soon rather than later. Life is short.

--

Lizzy's POV

The following morning, I woke up at 8. I wanted to start my box braids. Last night ended better than I expected. After everyone left the house and Mom and Mckenna went to bed, Cameron and I had a heart to heart. He heard me out and I had to do the same for him. I understood where his anger stemmed from. It came from feeling betrayed. Cameron looked up to dad as his role model and after he cheated he felt lost and like he had no one. He also felt like he had to carry the weight of the family since he was they only guy surrounded by 3 females. It was tough on him and I understood. I was glad when I got him to understand that people make mistakes and that life is very short. Slowly but surely, Cameron was going to try to forgive.

I cut and teased the braiding hair. I wanted poetic justice braids and wanted them a bit big. I sat on a chair in front of my dresser and braided. The one thing I hated about braiding my hair was that I would find the synthetic hair all over the place and all over my body. Like foreal I would find them in my pants and all over my butt. It's annoying.

I remember during my first year as a West, my mom asked me how I wanted to style my hair for picture day at school. I told her I wanted braids and she was so confused she called up every salon in town and one finally directed her to a hair braider. She took me to get my box braids and they turned out nice, but they were expensive. My mom didn't mind at all, but after getting it done a couple of times I didn't want to cost my mom so much money. When I was 12, I watched a ton of youtube videos and learned how to braid on myself. So that's what I have been doing for the past few years.

It was 11:30 when my phone rang. I had done almost the entire bottom half of my head but still had the top section to go.

"Hey, Ben." I said.

"Hey.Wanna go see a movie this afternoon?" He asked.

"I'm braiding my hair." I said.

"We can go a little later in the afternoon. Like 3?"

"I am braiding my hair." I repeated. There was a pause. "Ben." I said to make sure he was still on the line.

"Yeah....Didn't you just braid your hair the other day? It looked nice, why are you braiding it again." He sounded entirely confused.

"These are different braids." I explained. "They are box braids and they take a while."

"Alright." He said and I felt really bad. He wasn't understanding the fact that getting your braids done is a lengthy process, especially when you do it by yourself.

"I'm sorry. I'm sure Cameron will be happy to go with you. You can come over until then."

Ben chuckled. "No, you're fine, Lizzy. I'll be over in a bit."

I kept braiding after I hung up the phone with Ben. After 5 minutes I sighed as I dropped my arms down. They were starting to ache and my fingers were starting to cramp up. I was stretching my shoulders and suddenly froze when I noticed in my dresser mirror that Ben was leaning against my door frame with his arms crossed over his chest. He had an amused expression on his face which meant that he was intrigued or curious about something. I knew he was perplexed about my braids.

"Wow." Was all he said. "You weren't kidding when you said it would take a while." I just laughed and walked over to him and gave him a hug. He touched my braids and said, "There's a sale at the mall today."

My ears perked up. "Did you say sale?"

"Yes, we should go."

I pointed at my head which was only half braided. "I refuse to go out in public looking like this."

Ben took the snapback he was wearing off of his head and put It on my head. "Problem solved. Can't even tell that you're not done."

"Nice try, but no." I said placing his snapback on his head. He mumbled something with an annoyed expression on his face. "Um, what was that?" I asked. Ben just rolled his eyed. "Wha-did you just roll your eyes at me?" I asked shocked.

"I did. What are you going to do about it." Ben said challenging me by staring straight into my eyes.

I scoffed and crossed my arms over my chest. "I am not going anywhere with you."

Ben reacted by leaning down in front of me. I had no idea what he was doing until he lifted me off the ground and tossed me over his shoulder like a sack of potatoes and headed out of my room. "Hey! What are you doing? Put me down right now Benjamin Campbell!" Ben started walking down the stairs and my head bobbed up and down with each step he took. I tried to wiggle out of his grasp, but his arm held my legs firmly in place.

"If you keep moving I will drop you." Ben said. "Hold still." I heard him pull open the front door with one hand when we made it down the stairs. We were outside now and people probably think I was being kidnapped.

He walked across the street to his car and he put me in the passenger seat. Ben locked the door before I could even try to get out. I sat with my arm crossed over my chest as I waited from him to sit in the driver's seat. When he finally did, I said "You're annoying."

Ben turned the keys in the ignition and said, "Yeah I know you tell me atleast two times a day. This is nothing new."

"Ugh!" I said, and he patted the top of my half done head, and unfortunately this was kind of funny to me, but I tried really hard not to laugh. I failed and burst out laughing anyway and so did Ben. The laugh that comes when we realize we are both being over dramatic in the middle of a fight.

We went to the mall and they had a lot of pretty good deals. Ben wandered off into Hollister and I went to forever 21. I bought 2 tops and a dress and when I was done I went to sit on a bench out of Hollister to wait for Ben. After what happened the last time I went into that store I refused to set foot in there again.

I was just sitting there casually when this Black guy approached me. He looked to be about 18 years old and wore a Gucci belt and air force ones. His fade looked like his barber fell asleep mid fade and suddenly woke up, which made the fade entirely crooked and not straight. Is it really a fade if it isn't gradual? He stared at me and I stared back at him confused.

He licked his lips like he was ready to devour something. "Wow, you are really fine."

I rolled my eyes. "Leave me alone."

"Come on, don't be like that. You too pretty to be mean." He said.

"I'm also too pretty to be talking to you." I said. I was thinking I should just walk into Hollister and find Ben, but I really didn't want to go in there.

"You got a boyfriend?" The guy asked me. I ignored him. I also chose not to move because I didn't want him to think he was making me uncomfortable.

With perfect timing I saw Ben emerge from Hollister at the corner of my eye. One Hollister bag in his hand, and his eyes went from me to the guy standing in front of me. "Uh, you ready to go, Lizzy?"

"Yeah!" I said eagerly and stood up.

"Oh, really?" The guy said. "You go for white guys?"

"Shut up. And go fix your phony lookin fade." I said to him. I quickly grabbed Ben's arm. "Let's go."

Ben complied but was still confused. "Wait who was that?"

"I don't know."

"What have I told you about talking to strangers?" He said teasingly.

I hit him playfully. "Let's go home."

On the ride home, Ben kept checking his phone more frequently than he usually does, while he was driving. We got home and walked up the walkway to my front door.

"Here, I'll get the door." He hurried and went in front of me.

"Why are you being so weird today?" I asked.

He opened the door and I followed behind him. As soon as I walked in I was surprised beyond belief to see who was standing on the stairs smiling down at me.

"Jaden!" I screamed. I was not expecting to see him and my heart was so happy.

Chapter 23

"What..how...who?" I couldn't even form a complete sentence I was so shocked. Jaden jogged down the stairs and we embraced in a huge hug. "Did you get taller?" I noticed he was getting really tall.

"I think so." Jaden grinned at me.

I gasped. "Your voice is deeper. You hit puberty too!"

He chuckled. "Surprise." He said.

I turned to Ben. "Wow so this is why you kidnapped me?"

"Look I'm sorry I had to forcefully get you out of the house, but you were being too difficult." Ben said.

I went over and hugged him. "Thank you for this."

"Me? No, this was all Cameron's idea." Ben explained.

I looked at him confused and noticed Cameron at the corner of my eye leaned up against the wall. I was actually surprised because the whole brother and Jaden thing seemed to make Cameron jealous and feel replaced.

I let go of Ben and walked over to Cameron. "You planned this surprise for me?" I asked. Cameron smiled and simply nodded. "Thanks so much, Cam. It means a lot to me." I hugged him.

"This was really last minute planning. I got Jaden's mom's number from Ben and called her up this morning. I asked if he could spend the week with us since we have the same spring break this week. She eagerly said yes and I left early this morning to go pick him up." Cameron explained. "I needed Ben to get you out of the house for a bit so I could get things ready. He was great at stalling you."

"Cameron is really cool, Lizzy." Jaden said.

"We got the chance to bond on the drive over here." Cameron went and put his arm around Jaden. "It's like looking at you with a nice fade, Lizzy. You two could be twins." I laughed. "Mom literally bawled her eyes out when she saw him."

"You two can catch up." Ben said. "Cameron and I will be around."

I nodded and remembered my hair was still half slay and half struggle at the moment. "Come on up with me, Jaden. I just need to finish braiding my hair."

We went up to my room. I went back in front of my dresser to continue braiding while Jaden plopped down comfortably onto my bed and gazed around my room.

"You have a really nice house and family, Lizzy." Jaden said admirably.

"Yeah, they are pretty great." I said.

"Your parents must be loaded, because this house is massive."

I chuckled. "Well, I mean I wouldn't say loaded."

"Compared to where Auntie Ella and I live..."

I stopped mid braid and turned around to face him. "What did you just call her?" I asked. I knew last time I saw him, it was clear he didn't know the history of who his adoptive mother really was.

"I know now, Lizzy. She finally told me. After 10 years, she finally told me who she really is."

"I'm sorry. What was your reaction? How did you feel when she told you?" I knew it must have been difficult to grasp.

Jaden shrugged. "I don't know. I mean, I should have known. I was mad she kept it from me, but I guess she had good intentions. She raised me. She hasn't bothered to date or even get married and have her own kids. She has always focused on taking care of me. She's a good mom."

"You're really mature, you know that?" I said continuing to braid.

"You are too." Jaden stood. "Oh, and I told you so." He said.

"Told me what?"

"I knew Ben would be your boyfriend eventually." He giggled and I did too.

"Yeah, I was not expecting that to happen." I explained as I parted a piece of my hair with a comb.

"Well, I'm glad. I like him a lot."

"He is a really good guy. He's good to me." I said and just the thought of Ben made me smile.

Jaden and I continued to catch up until I finished braiding my hair.

Ben's POV

Cameron really stepped up this time. He knew he needed to get his act together and come to terms with issues he has been dealing with internally. I knew in the beginning, when Lizzy found Jaden, Cameron felt some type of way because he didn't want to lose Lizzy as his sister or being her brother. He also realized he pissed Lizzy off last night. He pushed all pride aside wanted to make it up to her. Cameron also knew that he had to meet his sister's biological brother.

As Jaden and Lizzy went to catch up Cameron and I went to his room to hang out.

Cameron sat at his desk and shook his head. "On the ride home with Jaden I just felt so...so comfortable talking to him. It's like I've known him for years. I know it's probably because of being around Lizzy, but...I can't believe he's only twelve. He speaks so maturely, like Lizzy."

"That kid is really awesome." I said.

"He is." Cameron spun around in his desk chair. "He was telling me about how he just found out his mom is really his aunt. How insane is that? He is an only child and has no dad around." Cameron paused as if he just realized something and sighed. "I am truly a terrible person. This kid doesn't even have an option of having a dad and I treat my own like crap."

I picked up Cameron's fidget spinner off his bed and played with it. "Bingo." I said.

Just then a knock came at the bedroom door and Jaden walked in. "Hey." He said.

"Hey, man." I said. "Coming to hang out with the guys now?"

He chuckled. "Yes. It gets boring with me and my mom." Jaden sat next to me on Cameron's bed.

"Hey are you sure you and Lizzy are related?" Cameron asked.

"Yeah." Jaden laughed. "Why?"

"Well you're a really sweet dude and Lizzy...well...she has a kick to her. She bites." We all burst out laughing.

I came at Lizzy's defense. "Look, Lizzy can be really sweet, but if you push one of her buttons she can snap." I explained. She's like a sour patch kid. She comes off as intense when you first meet her.

Jaden had a thoughtful expression on his face and chewed at his bottom lip. Just the way Lizzy did when she was in deep thought. Cameron must have noticed it too because he asked, "What are you thinking about, little dude?"

"I'm twelve, not two." Jaden snapped.

Cameron raised his arms up like he was surrendering. "Oh shit, nevermind. You definitely are Lizzy's brother."

Jaden chuckled. "I was just thinking about how cool it would be to have brothers or a brother."

"But you do have a brother. I'm your brother, Jaden. I'm Lizzy's big brother therefore I am yours too." Cameron said.

"I can be your other big brother too." I put my arm around Jaden affectionately.

Jaden grinned up at me. "Brother in-law, right?"

I chuckled. "You're a funny guy."

"We are both your big brothers. Anything you need, girl advice, guy advice, puberty advice, just let either of us know. Need a guys hang out? Tell us."

Cameron said. "I too have always wanted a brother. I will drive up to your house. I don't mind." He smiled.

"Thanks. You two are awesome." Jaden said while smiling.

Lizzy walked into the room. "What are you guys up to?" She asked with a smile across her beautiful face. She looked gorgeous with her finished braids.

"Just talking." Jaden said.

"Hey, let's go to the movies. That new Spiderman movie is out." I said as I stood up.

"Oh yeah that would be fun. I'll go get my-" Lizzy began but Cameron cut her off.

"Um, sorry Liz, but this is going to be a guys hang out. No girls allowed." Cameron said and walked out of the room. Jaden followed after him.

Lizzy's jaw dropped as she stared in disbelief. I walked past her and kissed her forehead and said, "Sorry babe. Bros night."

"Unbelievable." She mumbled, but forced an enthusiastic. "Have fun."

The three of us hurried out the door and piled into Cameron's BMW.

Lizzy's POV

Cameron, Ben, and Jaden all ditched me and went to the movies. I wanted to be annoyed, but I really couldn't. Jaden seemed to be having so much fun with them and I knew he must have needed some guy time with them. They would probably play in the arcade for an hour before the movie started. My mom went out with her girlfriends so I was left at home with Mckenna. I called Taylor over so the three of us could watch a movie.

"Wanna order a pizza?" I asked.

"Yeah! Pizza!" Mckenna exclaimed.

I called and ordered the pizza and they said it would take an hour to be delivered since there was a storm coming. It was spring so rain and heavy winds was common here. We went into my mom's master bedroom and sprawled on her bed to watch on her flat screen TV she had on the wall. She never mind if we wanted to watch movies in there.

We were 15 minutes into watching Moana, when a loud clap of thunder boomed outside. Suddenly the light in the hallway shut off. It was pitch black inside the house at this moment. I slid off the bed and looked outside the window. The street lights were still on so I assumed our power was the only one that went off in the neighborhood. I walked back to the bed and froze when I heard a noise downstairs.

"Did you hear that?" I asked Taylor. She made a facial expression seemed like she was trying hard to hear something. I paused the movie.

"No, I don't-" She began but was cut off when we heard glass breaking downstairs. 'M-maybe it's the pizza guy?" She said sounding afraid.

"A pizza guy that breaks into houses instead of ringing the doorbell? It's only been 20 minutes they said it would take an hour. My mom is out and the boys have to still be watching the movie." I said.

The sound of multiple footsteps came from downstairs and my heart began to beat fast. "I'm scared." Mckenna whimpered and Taylor hugged her closely.

"O-okay. I'll go downstairs and see." I whispered.

"No!" Taylor hissed. "What if they are burglars and have guns?"

"Stay with Mckenna. If I take too long or something just call the cops." I said. I took a deep breath walked into the hall way. I got on my hands and knees and crawled into Cameron's room to get his baseball bat, my only weapon for self defense.

I carried the bat over my shoulder as I walked slowly down the stairs to let my eyes adjust to the darkness. It felt like I was in a scary movie and being the idiot who goes to see what's going on and ends up killed. I walked through the darkened foyer and down the hallway to the kitchen slowly. As soon as I was about to enter the kitchen a dark figure came into view. I screamed and swung at the person, hitting his back. He groaned in pain as I continued to blindly swing. I grunted as I forcefully used my energy to smack with the bat.

With his arms shielding his face he said, "Hey! Hey! It's me! It's me!" The familiar voice cried out.

Just like clockwork, the lights in the house flickered on and I could clearly see Ben standing in front of me. I gasped. "OH MY GOODNESS! I am so sorry, Ben." I said, but Ben just looked at me like I was insane.

"What's going on?" Cameron said as he and Jaden emerged from the basement. He held a flashlight in his hand.

"I was just attacked by my girlfriend with a baseball bat. No big deal." Ben said.

"I thought you were an intruder!" I exclaimed. "Why are you guys home so early? You're supposed to be at the movies."

"Tickets were sold out. We waited in line forever, only to be disappointed. We hung out in the arcade a bit though and decided to come home since the weather was getting nasty. When we got home the power went out and I was looking for a flashlight in the junk drawer and accidently knocked over a glass that was on the counter. I went down into the basement with Jaden to check the fusebox." Cameron explained.

"Oh..oh" I said resting my palm on my forehead. "You guys scared us so much." The sound of police sirens and flashing blue and red lights interrupted our conversation and I groaned. "Oh no. Taylor must have called the cops when she heard me scream."

"Calling the cops is like her thing." Ben said. We all went to the front door and opened it, only to see two police officers on top of a guy in our front lawn handcuffing him. That guy was our pizza guy. Poor fella. The pizza box lay spread out with slices on the grass beside him. They thought he was the intruder.

"Well damn, no pizza for us." I said sounding disappointed.

--

After sorting things out with the police and pizza guy, they agreed not to charge us for calling them and they bought us a new pizza. It was such an eventful night. After we all ate pizza and left Mckenna to finish watching Moana in mom's room, Taylor went home. It was late and mom was still out with friends. I went back to check on Mckenna and realized she fell asleep on mom's bed. I gently carried her into her room and tucked her into bed.

I put on my pajamas which were actually just shorts an oversized t-shirt. Ben was sleeping over so the three boys could have a sleep over in Cameron's room. I walked quietly to his room to see that they were all fast asleep. I noticed how adorable it was. Ben and Cameron slept on the floor, while Jaden slept on Cameron's bed. I absolutely loved how they treated Jaden with such great care. It was the sweetest thing. I had to take a picture on my phone. I realized I was blessed to have amazing men in my life, two awesome brothers and an awesome boyfriend. I was even happier that Jaden was now a part of my life and my family.

In that moment, my life felt perfect.

Chapter 24

Spring break went by so fast, but it was very memorable and special for me. Jaden spent the entire week with us and it was very emotional for all of us when it was time for him to go back home. I promised him that we would all visit him soon.

It was Monday morning and the first day back after spring break. I woke up not feeling good, but had to suck it up. I had a chemistry exam today. My teacher is wicked because having an exam the first day back is cruel. I got dressed, threw my braids up in a bun and headed out the door. Walking past my new car and thinking about how useless it was because my best friend and boy friend lived in a 200 foot radius from me anyway. There really wasn't many places for me to go.

I stopped at the sidewalk and waited for Ben to emerge from his house. It was spring and the mornings were chilly and then it got warm as the day went on. I had my navy blue hoodie tied around my waist but took it off to wear it instead. As I was slipping it on, a sharp pain pierced my stomach. I froze waiting for the pain to subside before putting my hoodie on all the way. What was that? I thought. I tried not to make any subtle movements for fear of initiating more pain. When I didn't feel anything else I just shrugged it off and I watched as Ben's front door opened and he stepped out and jogged over to me.

"Hey, goodmorning." He said breathlessly as he gave me a kiss and threw his arm over my shoulder as we began walking in the direction of the school.

"Goodmorning." I said putting my arm around his waist. "How are you?"

"I'm good." Ben said in an upbeat tone. "And you?"

"I'm good too." I lied. I don't know why, but I was feeling like crap, but didn't want to worry Ben.

"You don't sound very good." Ben looked down at me with a suspicious look. "Hm, you miss Jaden, right?" I'll go with that. I did miss Jaden, but that definitely wasn't why I felt like just crawling into bed and going back to sleep.

I forced a laugh and said. "Yeah, I do miss him."

I felt Ben pull me closer to him and squeeze me tight. "We will make a trip down and see him soon, Okay?" Ben said reassuringly and kissed the side of my head.

I smiled. "Okay."

When we got to school everyone was chatting away about how their break went. Ben came with me to my locker to get the books I needed. I dropped my backpack on the ground in front of me and spun my combination. I opened the locker and reached in for my textbook and as soon as I did the sharp pain came back. I gasped because the pain took me by surprise.

"Lizzy, what's wrong?" Ben asked looking all over my face as if it contained the explanation for my sudden outburst.

"Nothing. " I lied. "It's probably just cramps. I think my period is coming." I said this even though I knew it was way too early for my period to come, but I couldn't think of any other explanation for my stomach pain.

Ben softened his concerned expression. "Oh, sorry, sorry." He rubbed my back affectionately. One thing I loved about Ben was that he wasn't easily grossed out. Heck, I don't think anything grosses him out. He was fascinated with the human body and I think that was his drive for becoming a surgeon one day.

I bent over trying to shove my book into my back pack, but Ben took it from me ."Here, I got it, Liz." He said placing it into my back pack, zipping it up, and tossing my back pack onto one of his shoulders to carry for me. Ben was such a gentleman. I held his hand as we walked to our first period class together. He rubbed small circles on the back of my hand which made me feel a bit better. I honestly don't know how I made it through the rest of the day.

I was able to sit through my chemistry exam without yelping in pain, but still felt crappy and wanted to go right home after school. The only problem was I still had to tutor Erin. Mr. Johnson said it would be good to go over any problems on the exam she struggled with.

I think Ben picked up on my sluggish mood because he said he would go back home and get his car to pick me up when I was finished. I didn't object to his request.

I sat across from Erin at the large, wooden, rectangle table in the library. I sighed. "How did the exam go for you?" I asked her.

She was chewing on a piece of bubble gum and twirled her blonde hair around her index finger. "It wasn't too bad. There was one question though..." She had a thoughtful expression on her face. "It was like something about gas laws." She said not really recalling the question.

I remembered the exact question she was talking about and wrote it out for her on a sheet of paper with each of the gas laws written at the top. "Okay, now read the question again and see if it makes sense and try to answer it." I said sliding the sheet of paper across the table. While she was figuring it out, I took that opportunity to put my head down. I just wanted to cuddle up with Ben right now.

I heard Erin clear her throat to get my attention. I sighed and raised my head up. Erin slid the paper across the table to me. I looked at it quickly. "Nice job." I said.

Erin just stared at me with narrowed eyes suspiciously. "Are you sick?" She asked.

"Why?" I asked feeling confused as to why she would even be concerned.

"Because it's been eighteen minutes into our session and you haven't insulted me yet." Erin said. "It's unusual. Something must be wrong with you."

"I'm fine." I said flatly. "Do you have any other questions from the exam?"

"Not that I remember them." She studied her chipped bright red nail polish.

"Cool, we can just end early for today." I said packing up my things and eager to get away from Erin.

"Alright." She said as she shut her chemistry textbook. "Hey, Lizzy?" She asked. "Can i ask you a dumb question?"

"You just did." I said and stared at her. "What?" I asked in annoyance.

"Have you tutored a lot of people before?"

"Not like this, why?" I said slowly zipping up my backpack.

"You're actually...good....at it." Erin said as if she had to forcefully make those words come out of her mouth.

I let out a small laugh. "Thank you?" I said it more as a question than a statement, because she sucked at giving compliments. She seemed like the one who was rather sick.

"Mhm..sure whatever." Anddd we are back to regular scheduled bitchy Erin programming.

I stood up. "I teach my little sister so she gets ahead in school. That's probably how I find the patience to teach you."

"Wait you have a sister?" Erin looked up at me surprised and oblivious to my slight insult. "Is she white or black..." He voice trailed off.

"Does it matter?" I snapped at her dumb question.

"No..it doesn't..I just meant..." She spoke hesitantly.

"Bye, Erin." I said walking away from the table. Ben was already outside when I was finished. We went over to my house and I told him I just wanted to cuddle and he was happy to. No one was home so we were alone. Ben and I were laying on my bed just relaxing and we began to kiss.

He moved on top of me. I had his face cupped in my hands. Randomly, he stopped kissing me and looked at me funny. "Are you feeling okay, Lizzy?" He asked.

"Um, yeah." I said and pulled his face closer to mine again so we could continue kissing. We kissed a little bit more before Ben pulled away and looked at me again.

His eyebrows furrowed with concern as if he was searching my face for something. "You're starting to burn up, Lizzy. I can feel it from kissing you. You have a fever." Ben said concerned.

Dating someone who is so medically intrigued can be annoying sometimes .I moved him off of me and sat up. "I mean, I have been feeling kind of crappy since morning." I said.

"Have you eaten?" Ben asked.

"No, I haven't really had an appetite at all today." I explained. "My stomach hurts and I know it's not my period." I admitted.

"Are you constipated?" Ben asked.

I laughed nervously. "We are not doing this."

"Doing what?" Ben asked.

"We are not gonna talk about my bowels." I said flatly.

"I really don't mind."

"I really do."

Ben looked at me and sighed. " Well, you should try to eat something."

I grimaced as I felt a sharp pain in my abdomen. "Okay, I will." I said.

"And tell your mom." Ben added.

"I'll do that too, Dr. Oz." I stood up and instantly regretted doing so when the room started to spin. I felt so dizzy. What is wrong with me?

"You good?" Ben asked as he slid off my bed and stood next to me.

"Yeah." I lied and started walking but was off balance and stumbled into Ben.

"You need to eat something right now, Lizzy. You look pale." Ben said and I literally stared at him in utter confusion for 10 seconds.

"I'm black... how in the hell do I look pale?" I asked.

"You aren't even dark." Ben answered. I guess he had a point. I was somewhere between light skinned and medium skinned, but more on the medium skinned side. I still did not see how Ben thought I looked pale.

"Whatever." I managed to say while feeling like I was on the verge of sudden death.

Ben turned with his back facing me and bent down. "Here." He said motioning for me to get on his back. Ben gave me a piggyback ride down the stairs and into the kitchen. "You're sick and you still have enough energy to argue. Amazing." Ben said as I sat down at the table.

"I think my energy is officially done for the today." I said. My head started to ache and I grimaced when sharp pain rain across my abdomen and lingered on the right side. Ben reheated up some left over baked pasta in the microwave and put it in front of me. I picked up the fork and tried to get some of it up to my mouth but I was feeling so weak all of a sudden.

"You need to see a doctor." Ben said taking the fork from my hand and feeding me. Even chewing was a lot of work. I really had no appetite. "Like right now." He added.

"Tomorrow. I'll go. I probably won't go to school. I'll tell my mom when she gets home." I managed to say. "I'm just tired right now. I think I'll go to sleep early."

Ben felt my forehead and neck with the back of his hand. "I can't leave you here alone by yourself." He brought another fork full of pasta to my mouth, but I shook my head 'no'. I was done eating.

"I'll be fine. I'm just gonna lay down. I feel kind of better after eating something." I said and forced a smile. "Thank you. Go home, I'll be okay."

Ben looked at me for a long time before saying , "Here, I'll get you to bed."
He carried me back upstairs and tucked me into bed. It was 8:30. Ben sat
at the edge of my bed as I lay there feeling miserable. "Seeing you sick is
depressing." He said.

I chuckled. "I'll be okay. I just need to rest. Go home. You have school
tomorrow." I said as I contemplated not going at all.

Someone jogged up the stairs and walked into my room. It was Cameron.
Ben quickly kissed my forehead. "I'll call you in the morning to see how
you're doing. Don't be sick, okay? I miss my Lizzy."

I chuckled softly. "Okay, I'll try."

Ben left my room and I heard him telling Cameron about how awful I
was feeling. I heard Ben's heavy footsteps jog down the stairs and then
Cameron walked into my room.

"How are you feeling?" Cameron asked.

"Like crap." I said. "I'm going to sleep now."

Cameron walked back out of my room and said, "I'll leave the door open.
Shout if you need anything."

I don't know how long I had been asleep, but the touch of a cold, wet towel
on my forehead woke me up. I opened my eyes and saw my mom sitting at
the edge of my bed looking down at me worried.

"Hey honey." She gave me a weak smile. "Sorry for waking you up. I'm
trying to get your temp down. It's at 104." She said as she moved the towel
to my neck and chest.

I felt the sharp pain in my abdomen again, but this time it was excruciating
pain. I slowly sat up in bed and as soon as I did I felt extremely nauseous.
I jumped out of bed and ran to the bathroom. I threw up. The little pasta

Ben fed me earlier was now in the toilet. I heaved twice and then started dry heaving because there was nothing left in my stomach. This pain and the other pain in my stomach mixed together was horrible. I started crying because the pain was unbearable.

My mom came into the bathroom and then a shirtless Cameron who was rubbing his eyes from sleep walked in with Mckenna by his side. "Lizzy! Lizzy! What's wrong?" She came close to me and started crying. Cameron pulled Mckenna back and put his arm around her to comfort her. She was so scared and to be honest I was too.

When the pain subsided, I flushed the toilet and stood up. After rinsing my mouth in the sink and my family staring at me in fear, the pain returned and I couldn't take it. The next thing I remember is everything going black. I passed out.

-

Comment what you guys think is wrong with Lizzy!

Chapter 25

BEN'S POV

Lizzy was on my mind the first thing when I woke up. I got ready for school quickly so I would have time to call her and see how she was feeling. When I did, her phone rang a couple of times, but she didn't answer. I called twice more and still no answer. Maybe she's sleeping. I decided to call Cameron instead to see how she was doing this morning.

"Ben." Cameron said in a serious tone first thing when he answered the phone.

"Hey, how's Lizzy feeling this morning?" I asked wandering around my room looking for my sneakers.

There was a pause before Cameron said, "My mom took her to the emergency room in the middle of the night. Her stomach was literally killing her and she started throwing up. It-it was bad...it was scary."

My heart started beating fast and I stopped abruptly in the middle of my room. "Is she okay? Have you talked to your mom?" Panic rose in my voice.

"Yeah, I talked to her about 2 hours ago. Lizzy went in for emergency surgery. It was appendicitis. Her appendix was inflamed." Cameron explained. "They said if she waited like 1 hour more...it wouldn't have been good, man." His voice shook as he spoke.

I let out a shakey breath and ran my fingers through my hair. "I'm heading to the hospital now then." I said.

"I seriously don't want to go to school, but I have a test 3rd period." Cameron said. "I have to drop Mckenna at day care too since my mom's still at the hospital."

"It's okay, can you grab both Lizzy and mines homework?" I asked as I removed my backpack off and tossed it onto my bed.

"Sure." He said.

I sped all the way to the hospital and a nurse guided me to the room Lizzy was in. When I walked in I saw Lizzy's mom sitting at the corner of the room looking exhausted.

She looked at me and tucked a strand of her blonde hair behind her ear. "Hey sweetie." She said with a tired voice and weak smile.

"Hey Ms. West." I looked over at Lizzy who was asleep in the hospital bed.

"She just got back from surgery. Just waiting for her to wake up." She shook her head as she looked at Lizzy lovingly. "My poor baby. I can't believe she didn't tell me sooner. This had to have started bothering her atleast over a day ago. She can be so stubborn sometimes."

I chuckled. "Yeah, she can be, but I know she just doesn't like to be a burden to others. She took a whole exam yesterday and probably aced it." Lizzy was the epitome of badass when it came to academics.

Ms. West smiled and shook her head. "She's a warrior." She sighed and looked at Lizzy admirably and said, "We left home last night in such a hurry. I need to go home and grab a couple things, but I don't want to leave her." Ms. West brushed a strand of her blonde off her forehead and said, "Seeing her in that much pain..again."

"Don't worry, I won't leave her side. I'll stay right here. Go do whatever you need to do." I said.

"Oh thank you, hun." She stood up and hugged me. "I'm so glad Lizzy has you." Lizzy's mom grabbed her purse, kissed Lizzy's forehead before rushing out of the room. I spent the rest of the time patiently waiting for Lizzy to wake up.

Lizzy's POV

I saw her vividly. So vividly it was like I could smell her.

I was engulfed in an abyss of pure white and my biological mother stood in front of me with a smile on her face. Her hands were clasped together right below her chin and joy in her eyes.

"Where am I?" I asked. "Wha-am..am I dead?" Panic filled my voice.

"No baby, you're not." She still had a smile plastered on her face. Her long black hair hung past her shoulders.

"Where am I?" I asked again." Why do I have all my senses?"

Without even answering my question she touched my face and said, "I love you and Jaden so much. We are so proud of you two for finding eachother."

"We?" I asked completely confused.

Just then my biological dad came in to view and was right beside my mom. "Yes, we are finally at peace. Keep him and that boy close to you, too. He is a good one and I approve." He smiled. Suddenly they both faded away.

"No wait come back." I pleaded but it was no use. They faded from my view. My parents were gone. That's when I heard it. A beeping noise.

I'm dying. I am dying. This is it.

I slowly opened my eyes. I was in an unfamiliar room and I was confused. The rhythmic sounds coming from the heart monitor jolted my memory. Then I remembered what happened last night. The pain, the vomiting, passing out, and coming to the hospital. I remember getting an ultrasound and the doctors telling me I had appendicitis before taking me into surgery for an appendectomy. It all came flooding back.

I felt pain in my stomach still, but it was a different kind of pain. It was more of a sore feeling. I scanned the entire room and my eyes landed on Ben sitting in the corner scrolling through his phone. Waking up and seeing him first made me forget where I was and also made remember what my biological father said.

He's a good one and I approve.

"Ben." My voice came out hoarse and as a whisper so I knew Ben couldn't hear me. My mouth felt dry. I tried to clear my throat but using my abdominal muscles made my stomach hurt, but I repeated his name again. "Ben.."

He heard me this time and his eyes looked up from his phone and lit up. He stood up excitedly and walked over to me. "Hey there, Beautiful." He kissed my forehead and smiled at me. "Hey." He whispered as he caressed my left cheek with his thumb and his face inches away from mines.

I smiled and said. "Hey."

"How are you feeling?" He asked.

"I'm okay. Just a little sore." I looked down at my arms which were hooked up to a million things.

"Push the little pump." Ben reached over me and grabbed this small little remote looking thing. "It'll give you some pain killers through your arm. I pressed it and expected instant relief, but I knew life didn't work that way.

I gave Ben a weak smiled and said, "Thanks." I touched his hand. "How long have you been here?"

"For like an hour and a half." Ben said. "I've been doing some research on appendicitis. We should have just WebMDed your symptoms yesterday." He shook his head.

"I'm sorry, I should have listened to you and went to the doctor yesterday. I just-"

"Shh, shh. It doesn't matter anymore, Lizzy. What matters is you're okay now." Ben grinned at me. "I'm gonna call your mom and tell her you're awake. She just needed to go home to take care of somethings." I nodded in understanding and watched as Ben walked to the corner of the room to make the phone call.

Just then a nurse walked into the room. She had on bright pink scrubs and short brown hair. Her voice was cheery and a bit annoying. "Hello! My name is Jenny. I'll be your nurse." She glanced at the monitor "Blood pressure looks really good." She walked over to me. "Can you tell me your name and date of birth, hun?"

"Elizabeth West." I said. "September twenty-fifth."

"Good! Doctor Ramirez should be in shortly to check on you. Can I get you anything?" Jenny asked in an upbeat voice.

"Um..can I have water please and another blanket. I'm freezing." I said.

"No problem." She said. 5 minutes later she brought me back water and a heated blanket. Soon after that the doctor came in to see me.

"Hello there, Elizabeth. How are you feeling?" He asked.

"Alright." I said.

"Let me take a look at your abdomen." He said as he lowered my bed and raised my hospital gown.

Ben was off the phone and came and stood directly behind him and looked at my stomach in fascination before smiling, nodding his head and saying "nice". The doctor turned and gave him a confused look. "Oh don't mind me. Just in love with surgery, that's all." Ben explained.

"My boyfriend wants to be a surgeon. Just like you." I told the doctor.

The doctor chuckled. "You will definitely love it. You should come and shadow me some time."

"Really?" Ben's face lit up. "The closest things to surgery I've seen is 12 seasons of Grey's Anatomy. So that would be great!"

Dr. Ramirez chuckled again and said, "Yeah, just let me know." He said. The doctor felt the right side of my belly and said, "Looks good, Elizabeth. Have you eaten anything since the surgery?" He asked and I shook my head. "Order something to eat.

"Okay, thanks doc." I said.

"Thank you." Ben said as he shook the doctor's hand before he left the room.

I ordered some rice with chicken and mashed potatoes. Fifteen minutes later my food was brought to me by a tall, thin man with curly blonde hair.

"Enjoy." He said as he walked out of the room. Enjoy? How does a patient enjoy hospital food? I lifted the top off the tray of food and looked at the plate in disappointment. I smelled it and it smelled okay. I ate a spoonful of mashed potatoes and gagged as I dropped my spoon onto the plate.

"I think I'm gonna be sick...again." I said looking at Ben.

Ben chuckled. "Is it that bad?" He came around to the other side of my bed. I fed him a piece of my chicken and watched him chew thoughtfully."It's not terrible." He finally said after eating it.

"What do you mean it's not terrible? There's no trace of seasoning in any of it." I sighed and I exclaimed and pushed the tray away from me in disgust. Sometimes I forget Ben is white and his idea of taste is different than mine.

"Oh, come on, Lizzy. Just eat it. You need something in your stomach." Ben said as he rubbed his thumb across my cheek. "Besides, this food is made for sick people."

"But it tastes nasty." I whined.

Ben tossed back his head and laughed. "Remember how Mckenna was acting like a brat on her birthday? Well you're being one right now too." He said and he was right. I couldn't even argue with him.

"Don't make me laugh." I said. "It hurts." I smiled up at him.

"I'm sorry." He said softly. "I promise to get you a ton of snickers when you're all better.

"Fine." I said and pulled the tray back to me and finished the entire meal. Snickers was all the motivation I needed.

Ben just patiently watched me eat with an amused expression on his face.

"Ben, have you eaten anything today?" I asked suddenly concerned.

Ben just shrugged. "No, but-"

I cut him off. "Please go to the cafeteria and get something." I said..

He played with one of my braids. "I want to stay with you. I don't want you to be lonely."

I smiled at him and rubbed his face with my thumb. "I'll be fine, Ben. Oh, and can you like get me a burger or a pizza?

Ben just smiled at me and said. "Okay."

"Wait really?" I asked shocked at how he didn't object to my request.

"Anything for you." Ben said as he leaned down and gave me a peck on the lips. "But of course not, Lizzy. You know you can't have food like that just yet" He added.

Just then my nurse, annoying Jenny, came in. "Hey! How are you?"

I rolled my eyed. "Still okay. Thanks." I said stiffly. She was literally disrupting my peace of mind.

Jenny looked at Ben and said "I'm Jenny, her nurse. I didn't get to meet you earlier." Her perky tone turned in a flirty one. She couldn't be any older than 22, but either way Ben was still way too young for her cougar self. "Are you a friend?"

"Boyfriend. He's my boyfriend." I said quickly to lay the facts straight to her.

Jenny's expression turned into a surprised one. "Oh! Boyfriend. Wow. Lucky girl." She grinned at me. "He's a cute one." She pretended to whisper to me and chuckled.

"I know." I said flatly and in no way humored.

"And can I get you anything?" She asked him.

Ben chuckled nervously. "No, I'm good, thanks."

"You sure?" She asked.

"He said he's good." I reiterated. "Thank you, Jenny." Irritation filled my voice.

"Just call me if you need anything." She said as she walked out of the room and winked at Ben.

"What was that?" Ben asked as he stared after the nurse in utter confusion.

"Don't tell me you didn't notice her flirting with you, Ben." I said as I rolled my eyes.

"Of course I noticed. That was just plain disrespectful. " He glanced up at the heart monitor screen and said, "Your blood pressure shot up, Lizzy." His expression turned serious.

"It was her. She is detrimental to my health. I need a new nurse." I crossed my arms over my chest annoyed and realized how bratty I was being and quickly uncrossed them.

Ben just grinned at me and said, "Relax. I'm all yours." He gave me a two short pecks on the lips and looked back at the monitor. His kisses definitely made me feel more calm and I knew that if my blood pressure went up the doctor would probably want to keep me here longer than necessary. I couldn't be bothered by that slutty nurse.

At the corner of my eye I saw someone walk into the room. It was my dad. He was dressed in his business clothes and his blonde hair which now had streaks of gray looked disheveled like he ran all the way over here. His untied tie hung around his neck and the buttons on the top of his shirt were open revealing some of his chest hair. Basically he looked a hot mess.

"Oh, Honey." He walked over to me fast.

I looked at him in shock. "Dad? Wh-what are you doing here? " I was lowkey surprised because he lived over 2 hours away and managed to get here so fast.

He kissed my forehead. "I got here as soon as I could. I was at getting ready for work when your mom called me. How are you feeling?"

"Better than I did last night that's for sure. I'm fine, really." I chuckled and instantly regretted it. "Ouch." I said.

He called the nurse and Doctor into my room and asked them a million and one questions about me and the surgery and my recovery. After he was done interrogating them he stood next to my bed. My dad smiled and the creases next to his blue eyes deepened. "Take it easy." He patted my leg. "You've always been a real trooper, Liz." He then turned and looked, Ben. "Hey there kiddo. How are you?" He asked, finally acknowledging him since he was too frazzled earlier.

"I'm good." Ben said confidently.

My dad placed his hand on his shoulder. "Have you eaten? How about you and I go grab some lunch."

Ben's confidence dwindled away as panic ran across his face. "Oh, no I'm not hungry." He said nervously and I wanted to laugh so bad. He was clearly lying. Ben and my dad never exchanged more than five words. Ever. My dad could also be pretty intimidating when he wanted to be so I knew exactly what he was trying to do. I also felt bad for Ben because I knew he would feel awkward being alone with my dad and I couldn't blame him. He was rarely around.

"Don't be silly. Come on, let's go." My dad urged and Ben obliged looking uncomfortable.

"Don't have too much fun without me." I teased as they both walked out the door.

Ben's POV

Having lunch with Mr. West made me nervous for different reasons. One being the fact that I have barely talked to him before. Two being the fact that he was the father of my girlfriend so I figured he hated me just because.

Strangely enough, he was being nice to me. Extremely nice.

He paid for our food and we sat at table in the hospital cafeteria and ate in silence for a couple minutes before he spoke up and said, "I messed up."

I didn't wanna look up at his face so I focused most of my attention on my cheeseburger like it was the most interesting thing I've ever seen. I was trying to inhale it and eat fast so I could leave and go back up stairs to be with Lizzy.

"I made a huge mistake and it cost me my family. I would give anything to have my family back but now it's too late." He continued. "I can't change the past and what I've done. I hurt them so bad. My kids are my world. Lizzy is my world. My first daughter, my princess. She was a daddy's girl but now that's all changed. If you ever hurt her, I promise you will regret it."

I froze and finally looked at him after hearing his threat. "Yes, sir." I said and gulped.

Mr. West finally smiled. "I know that you're a good kid. Lizzy seems happy. I know Cameron wouldn't allow you two to be together if he didn't think you weren't good for her. He loves her so much." He sighed and said, "Do better than I did. I know you're a good one and I do approve."

I finally relaxed my body which was tense throughout the whole time I was eating. I felt relieved that Lizzy's dad didn't hate me, but he still intimidated me a lot.

We went back up to Lizzy's room but when we got there we were shocked to see the bed Lizzy was laying in empty.

"Lizzy?" Mr. West shouted loudly. "Lizzy?" He repeated again but this time he sounded worried.

Where could she have gone?